How to Get
The Body You Want
by Peony Pinker

First published 2011 by
A & C Black
Bloomsbury Publishing plc
50 Bedford Square
London WC1B 3DP

www.acblack.com

ISBN 978-1-4081-5237-9
A CIP catalogue for this book is available from the British Library.

This book is produced using paper that is made from wood
grown in managed, sustainable forests. It is natural, renewable and
recyclable. The logging and manufacturing processes conform
to the environmental regulations of the country of origin.

Printed and bound by CPI Group (UK) Ltd, Croydon, CR0 4YY

JENNY ALEXANDER

HOW to Get THE BODY YOU WANT

BY

Peony Pinker

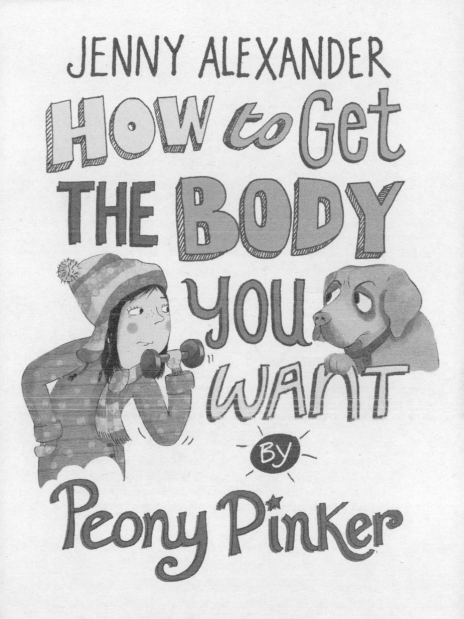

A & C Black • London

Contents

Chapter 1
The year that's gone and the year ahead

You know when your whole family goes out for lunch at the Happy Haddock on New Year's Day, and they talk about the best bits of the year that's gone and what they want to happen in the year ahead?

And you secretly think they've got as much chance of their wishes coming true as your rabbit, Dennis, would have of getting on Strictly Come Dancing?

Well that's what happened to me the first New Year that Gran was back in Polgotherick.

Her new house wasn't ready for her to move into yet because the builders were still sorting out the dry rot and stuff. It had been empty for years, standing all on its own out there on the cliff path, turning into a crumbly old ruin.

In the meantime, she was living in the Happy Haddock because it belonged to her old school-friend, Jane, and that was how come we were there for New Year's lunch instead of having our traditional frozen pizza. Why bother going out when you can easily pop a pizza in the oven? That's what Dad says.

The Happy Haddock overlooks the harbour and it's one of the oldest buildings in Polgotherick. It's got walls about a mile thick and tiny windows, so it's always dark inside, even in the middle of the day. There's a net of tiny twinkly lights across the black ceiling-beams that gives you the odd feeling you're moving around at the bottom of the ocean, with bright bubbles on the surface above.

The place was crammed. All the tables were squeezed up to make room for the Christmas tree. It was so noisy we had to almost shout to make ourselves heard.

'It's a good job we booked!' Gran said, as we bagged our table.

Dad went to get some drinks and nuts and order the food, and then we all sat round talking about the year that had gone by. When you came to think about it, amazing things had happened for each and every one of us.

'I became an agony aunt!' said Dad, and he had, well, sort of. He tried for a few weeks after Daphne, the real agony aunt, went missing, but then Mr Kaminski from next door ended up secretly doing it for him because he was so hopeless. Ed, the editor on the Three Towns Gazette, couldn't believe how good his sports reporter had turned out to be at sorting out people's problems.

'I also haff become agony aunt,' said Mr Kaminski.

'An undercover agony aunt,' agreed Gran.

You might be wondering what our next-door neighbour was doing at a family lunch but as he didn't have any family of his own, he had kind of adopted us. At the beginning of the year he had been like a sad old snail stuck in his shell, but doing the problem page for Dad and getting Mum to rescue his wreck of a garden seemed to have drawn him out.

'I can hardly believe it, but I actually set up my own business,' said Mum.

It was called Garden Angels and although it meant she was out from dawn to dusk trimming trees and digging flower-beds at least she wasn't spitting feathers any more about having to work for horrible Mr Pryce at the Green Fingers Garden Centre.

Going round the table, Gran said, 'I hung up my wetsuit in St Ives and came home to Polgotherick. No more surf-school teaching for me!'

Mr Kaminski beamed at her. He had been even more keen on us Pinkers since Gran had come back.

It was Primrose's turn but she was busy texting Matt and didn't notice. You could always tell it was him she was talking to because she got this gooey look when she read her messages and sighed every time she pressed send. I helped her out.

'Primrose managed to get a decent boyfriend for a change,' I said.

'And what about you, Peony?' said Gran.

I grinned at her. 'I got Dennis.'

I had never had a pet before, and I probably never would have if Gran hadn't suddenly decided that having a house rabbit might distract us from arguing all the time.

'Well, I'd say that was a pretty good year!' said Mum, and we chinked our glasses together.

'And here comes a great start to the New Year,' said Dad, as the waiter arrived with our fish and chips.

The sign outside the Happy Haddock says, 'The best fish 'n chips in Polgotherick', and it's true, though to watch Primrose picking at her fish as everyone else tucked in to theirs, you'd have thought there must be something grim and stinky lurking beneath the batter.

Mum shot her a frown. If we'd been at home she would have told her off about wasting food and being silly worrying about her weight, when she was perfectly normal and a lovely-looking girl. Then Primrose would have gone off on one, saying it was all very well for someone who had not mysteriously ballooned into a blob to say things like that.

In four weeks' time it was Matt and Primrose's six-month anniversary and they were planning to do the same things and wear the same clothes as they did on their first date. Unfortunately, when Primrose tried her dress on before Christmas, she discovered she had to choose between either doing it up or breathing.

Dad tried to distract Mum with the sauce basket but she spotted Primrose slipping a chip to Magnus, and gave her a double-strength glare. She couldn't say anything because she didn't want to spoil Gran's special lunch.

Dogs are supposed to look like their owners, but although Magnus is as round as an apple like Jane, he hasn't got her friendly face. Labradors are usually very well-behaved and sociable, but Magnus took Primrose's chip as if he was doing her a favour, and then scowled at her until she gave him another one. I thought Mum was going to explode.

It was annoying Primrose messing about with her food all the time but I was just as annoyed with Mum for getting in a stress about it. I mean, it wasn't as if Primrose was going to starve. Whenever she gets in a mood, which isn't exactly rare, she goes through the fridge like a walrus hoovering up clams. A walrus can eat four thousand clams in one sitting – I saw that on David Attenborough.

'Let's talk about what we want to happen in the year ahead,' said Dad. 'Who'd like to start?'

Gran said, 'Well, I'll be moving into Nash House, of course. Then I want to get my skipper's certificate so I can start doing boat trips round the harbour.'

'Is no need,' Mr Kaminski said. 'I haff skipper's certificate.'

'You can't always be there, Viktor,' said Gran.

'But yes,' he said. 'I can.'

Mr Kaminski said what he wanted in the year ahead was to help Gran with her boat trip business. I hoped he had some other wishes up his sleeve in case Gran got another of her big ideas and went off the boat trip thing. She had nearly abandoned it once already in favour of having a tea-room at Nash House, till Mum reminded her about the Great Bed-and-Breakfast Disaster. The problem with Gran is, she's easily distracted.

'Have you got any other New Year wishes?' Dad asked Mr Kaminski. Great minds think alike.

Mr Kaminski got embarrassed and muttered something in Polish. He said he did have another wish but he couldn't explain it in English.

'Vot about you, Jan?' he asked Mum, changing the subject.

Mum said she wanted to make her business really successful so she could take on more people and end up working less hours. Dad rolled his eyes.

'What?' said Mum.

'You working less? I don't think so!' said Dad.

Magnus nudged Primrose's elbow with his nose and she gave him another chip. Then Jane stopped wiping the bar with her tea-towel and called out, 'Walkies, Magnus!', so he waddled off. He's the only dog I've ever met who hears the word 'walkies' and hides.

'What about you, Primrose?' said Mum.

'She wants to try and hold onto Matt and not drive him away by being a drama queen,' I suggested, helpfully.

'Yes, and Peony wants to learn how to keep her beak out of other people's business,' said Primrose.

'What about you, Dave?' said Mum, moving swiftly on.

Dad drew himself up in his seat, paused until he had everyone's undivided attention, then made his big announcement.

'I'm going to write a book!'

We gawped at him. Writing a book sounded like quite a lot of effort for someone whose hobbies were watching sport on TV and snoozing.

'Ed says all the best agony aunts write a book,' said Dad. 'Daphne's was "How to Handle Stress at Work."'

'Oh, yes,' goes Mum. 'She wrote that just before she went on holiday and refused to come back!'

Dad said his book was going to be about fitness because lots of people who wrote to the problem page weren't happy with their bodies and it was a subject he knew about, having had a life-long interest in sport.

'But it doesn't have to be something *you* know about, does it?' Primrose said. 'I mean, it'll be Mr Kaminski who writes it, with Gran checking his English like she does with the problem page.'

It was a fair comment, given that Dad's favourite motto is, 'If a job's worth doing, it's worth getting someone else to do it.' But he insisted he had always wanted to write a book and this was his big chance.

'I am definitely going to do this myself!' he declared.

Our New Year's Day lunch seemed to be turning into the Mad Hatter's Tea Party, and when Gran pointed out that I hadn't come up with anything I wanted to achieve in the year ahead, I almost said about getting Dennis on Strictly.

They would have told me off for being silly, but just to sum up:

+ the person with the shortest attention span in the country was going to study for her skipper's certificate and set up a boat trip business without getting side-tracked by other ideas

+ the person with no Plan B was going to depend on her seeing it through

✦   the biggest workaholic in the world was going to build up her business but cut her hours

✦   the most outrageous drama queen in the galaxy was going to keep her boyfriend and not get into a strop and accidentally dump him (again)

✦   the laziest person in the whole entire universe was going to write a book even though he could easily get out of it

'I can't think of anything,' I said.

Gran squeezed some more ketchup on her chips and put the empty sachet on the edge of her plate beside the other five.

'It'll come to you,' she said.

Chapter 2
Windy walks and woolly sandwiches

On the second day of January every year, my friend Toby and his family have a picnic at Pike's Bluff. Mum says most people wouldn't even think of having a picnic in the middle of the winter and if they did, a windy cliff would be the last place they would choose for it.

Dad says most people wouldn't go to Pike's Bluff at all, it being about a billion miles down the coastal path and in the middle of nowhere. Anyone with an ounce of sense would walk to the first stile and then come back for tea and cakes in the Harbour cafe.

I'd never been as far as Pike's Bluff before so when Toby invited me, I said yes. I thought there must be some kind of shelter if they went there for winter picnics and it couldn't be as far as Dad said because Toby's little sister, Leah, had done it last year when she was only seven.

Toby's dad ran the Polgotherick Scouts and his mum ran the Guides. When you went on a day out with them it felt like you were going for your Survival Skills badge. They wore shorts all the year round, not beach-style shorts but knee-length ones with lots of pockets. Toby often did as well, which didn't do much for his cool-rating at school.

The only one in Toby's family not wearing shorts that day was Leah. She was well wrapped up, with tights and leggings under her skirt and a thick woollen hat, scarf and mittens.

It was freezing as we set off along the coast path. Our breath made clouds in the air. There was a dusting of snow on the ground and the grass crunched under our feet. Toby's dad took the lead, the hairs on his legs fluffed out in the cold. He had a massive back-pack and two strong walking-poles, as if he was planning to trek to Siberia.

Toby's mum walked just behind him, with me, Leah, Toby and Jess, our friend from school, bringing up the rear. Jess doesn't usually like outings and stuff but what with her dad walking out and everything, me and Toby were on a mission to try and cheer her up. By the time we reached the first stile I was already puffing and panting.

The path was very up-and-down, with wooden steps dug into the dirt on the steepest bits. I was struggling to keep up but Jess was even worse than me. She had never been on a day out with Toby's family before so she was probably in shock.

'Are they bionic?' she muttered, as we stumbled down a steep bit into a ravine and trudged back up the other side.

Toby's mum and dad were dots in the distance by the time we got to the old lookout so we didn't stop for a rest but pushed straight on.

'H-h-h-how far are we going?' puffed Jess.

'My dad says it's about a billion miles,' I said.

She groaned and flopped forward, resting her hands on her knees. Toby and Leah had gone ahead by then so they didn't notice.

'It's all right when you get used to it,' I said. 'You reach a stage when you think you're definitely going to die, then that kind of passes and you feel okay.'

'Yeah?' said Jess.

I gave her my best encouraging smile, the one your mum does when she's finished explaining the bit of homework you're stuck on.

We trudged on. From time to time Toby and Leah stopped to wait for us, but their mum and dad were nowhere to be seen.

'Don't worry,' goes Toby. 'You can't get lost up here.'

I had thought the path would go on being up-and-down all the way to Pike's Bluff, but after a while it hit a high bit and stayed there. The coast levelled out and the path, no more than a dip in the grass now, followed the line of the cliffs for as far as the eye could see.

Up here, we were suddenly hit by the wind. It blew in blasts straight in off the sea, buffeting us, making our hats flap and our chins tingle. It was exciting, like a blast of music on a funfair ride.

Toby turned his back to the wind, undid his coat and flung it open. He looked like a cormorant drying its wings. A gust of wind lifted him clean off his feet and he flapped and stumbled across the field, laughing hysterically.

We all joined in. We were like human kites, bumping across the frosty grass, trying to take off and never quite managing it. Eventually, Leah threw herself down on the ground, rolled onto her back and lay there laughing. We all flung ourselves down beside her.

'I'm not tired any more,' Jess said, in surprise.

'I told you,' I said.

Toby said it was just as well, considering we still had a bit of a way to go.

But it only felt like five minutes before we saw a sharp rise up ahead and a spur of cliff jutting out towards the sea. Big waves were breaking on the rocks below, and flecks of foam flew right up over the path like giant snowflakes on the wind.

'That's Pike's Bluff,' Toby said. The wind seemed to blow the words right out of his mouth, so we could hardly hear him.

'What, and we're going to have our picnic up there?' I shouted. There wasn't a stick of shelter.

Toby laughed.

'No – that would be nuts!'

Leah was walking ahead now, and she suddenly dropped out of sight, like she had fallen off the cliff. I screamed and broke into a run, but Toby grabbed my sleeve. He shook his head to say there was no need to panic.

As we got closer to the place where Leah had disappeared we saw that the cliff at this point wasn't as sheer. It was lumpy. It looked as if great chunks had fallen off and tumbled towards the water a billion trillion years ago, and then gone grassy.

Toby set off down a narrow dirt path that wound steeply down in front of us. Jess and me looked at each other. What was the point in clambering all the way down when there was nothing at the bottom but foam and rocks? But we couldn't stay up at the top on our own.

The path wasn't as frightening as it looked. When we got to the last bit, we suddenly saw a thin strip of sand right up against the bottom of the cliff that you couldn't see from the top. A secret beach! We speeded up.

The sand was criss-crossed by a few tracks where Toby's family had walked over it. His dad had made a fire at the far end under the cliff, and Toby and Leah were collecting drift-wood to keep it burning. The flames flew sideways in the wind.

Toby's mum called us over and we all sat down to eat our sandwiches. We didn't take our gloves off or our fingers would have frozen. The crumbs stuck to the wool, and the wool snagged on the crusts, so as well as the gritty crunch of sand you always get when you eat on the beach we also got the odd stringy bit of wool stuck in our teeth.

'Would you like to know five facts about Pike's Bluff?' asked Jess.

Jess collected facts like a squirrel collects acorns, stashing them away in her notebooks ready to bring out when the time was right. She said five was the perfect number of facts to find out – it was enough to make you feel you knew something worth knowing, but not so many that you got bogged down.

Jess told us her five facts and then we got to talking about the best picnics we'd ever been on. Jess and me realised we'd only ever had picnics in the summertime, and usually on the beach.

'My best one was on Hawk's Tor with hailstones as big as marbles bouncing off the rocks,' said Toby.

'But what about the time we rowed out to that little island?' Leah said.

'Or when we cycled across the fens and saw all those swans,' said their dad.

'I've never done anything like that,' said Jess.

Toby's mum said they were going up Snowdon in the Easter holidays. It was the highest mountain in England and Wales.

'Why don't you two come too?'

'We're going to get a tepee tent,' said Leah. 'There'll be lots of room.'

Jess looked surprised, but then she doesn't know Toby's family very well.

'You're camping – at Easter? Won't you freeze to death?'

'No, our tepee's going to have a fire in the middle. It's going to have a hole for the smoke to go through!' said Leah.

I was like a cat with a kipper for the rest of the day. I was soooo excited about going up a mountain and camping in a tepee.

But when I got home it was like someone snatched that kipper clean away. Mum and Primrose were in the kitchen having a massive row about Primrose refusing to eat her dinner.

'I can hardly do my dress up,' Primrose yelled. 'And it's all your fault!'

'Well, pardon me for slaving over a hot stove day in day out to give you a healthy diet!' yelled Mum. 'You're being stupid! Starving yourself is not the way!'

Dad appeared, looking for chips and dips. I could hear football commentary from the TV upstairs. It must be half-time.

'Save yourself,' he muttered to me, as he grabbed his snacks and hot-footed it back up to the living-room.

I glanced around for Dennis but he must have been hiding somewhere, and anyway I suddenly realised I was too tired to look for him. I hauled myself upstairs and pitched onto the sofa next to Dad.

I managed one chip before I fell asleep. I dreamt I was walking up a high mountain with Toby and Jess. I was wearing shorts with gazillions of pockets and all those pockets were full of stones. I could hardly lift my feet to put one in front of the other.

When I woke up I felt more tired than ever. My body seemed to have sunk into the sofa and got stuck. I actually couldn't move.

That's when it came to me – my New Year's resolution. I had to get a whole lot fitter before Easter. It would be just too terrible if Toby's mum and dad had to make a stretcher out of their sweatshirts and carry me back down the mountain because I collapsed in a heap half-way to the top and couldn't get up again!

Chapter 3
The family organiser and the four-week plan

'It's not like you to sleep so late,' Mum said the next morning, when I got downstairs.

She and Dad were sticking up the new family organiser on the kitchen wall. Other families have a calendar with pictures of scenery and stuff, and you turn to a new page every month. In our house, we have all the months printed off the web without any pictures, spread out over half a wall.

Dad says it's better that way because we can see the whole year at a glance, plus it covers up all the pinholes and cracks, so he doesn't have to decorate. Mum says it saves arguments because if she gets a nice calendar with gardens, someone (naming no names) is bound to say it isn't fair and why can't we have one with Hollyoaks instead?

They stood back to admire their work. January, February and March were way high because October, November and December had to be out of Dennis's reach or he would eat them. You can house-train your rabbit to use a litter tray for his pees and poos, but there's no way you can stop him munching up absolutely anything munchable he can get to.

'What colour smileys would you like this year?' Mum said.

I picked gold. We always put our own colour sticker next to the things we're doing. I put one on my birthday, then pushed a chair up so that I could get to March.

'Ouch!' I cried, trying to step up onto it. 'My legs hurt. There must be something wrong with them.'

Mum laughed.

'You're just stiff from your walk yesterday.'

'It'll soon wear off,' said Dad.

It didn't feel as if it would wear off. It felt as if my legs were seizing up and soon I wouldn't be able to walk at all.

I put my sticker on the Easter weekend, next to Mum's drawing of an Easter egg. Then I wrote, 'Snowdon' next to it.

'Snowdon?' goes Mum. 'What — the big mountain in Wales?'

'Yes. Toby's family are going to walk up it and they've invited me and Jess to go too.'

'Why are they going to walk up it?' Dad said. 'There's a perfectly good train that goes right the way to the top.'

'And where are you going to stay?' asked Mum. 'It's too far to go for a day, you know.'

I told them Toby's family were going to get a tepee. Dad said normal people only went camping in the summer, and Mum said we would probably catch pneumonia. I told her about the fire and chimney-hole but she said I must have got my wires crossed. You definitely didn't get fires and chimney-holes in tents.

'Ouch!' I stepped back down off the chair. Mum said if walking to Pike's Bluff had made my legs seize up, maybe climbing Snowdon might be a bit ambitious. Dad said there was plenty of time for me to get fit before Easter.

'Peony can help me test-drive my ideas for the book,' he said. 'We can do it together!'

'What?' goes Primrose, appearing at the bottom of the stairs, rubbing her eyes. 'Do what together?'

One of her pyjama legs was ruckled up round her knee and her hair looked as if a hyperactive mouse had been nesting in it. She groaned when she saw the family organiser. She blinked hard and stepped back as if it was an alien spaceship that had burst through our kitchen wall and she couldn't quite take it in. Talk about a drama queen.

'Sit down and I'll make you some breakfast,' Mum said, trying to steer her towards the table.

'I don't want any breakfast.'

Dad and me looked at each other. He raised one eyebrow.

'Breakfast is the most important meal of the day,' said Mum, in her most reasonable, teacher-type voice.

Primrose dropped down onto a chair and rolled her eyes, as Mum went through all the usual stuff about how crash-dieting could actually make you fat. If you starved yourself, she said, your body thought, 'Oh, no – times are tough – better lay down as much flab as possible before things get any worse!' Then every little bit you ate went straight onto your waist.

She said a bit of seasonal variation was normal. People were always slightly lighter in the summer months and heavier in the winter, so it wasn't surprising that Primrose's dress was a little bit tight at the moment.

'Give it a few months and you'll be back in that dress, no bother!' said Mum.

Primrose suddenly woke up like one of those monsters that sleep for hundreds of years until someone disturbs them, and then they go nuts.

'I haven't got a couple of months!' she said.

She jumped up, grabbed a red smiley and jabbed it onto the family organiser at the beginning of February. She snatched the pen out of my hand and wrote, 'Six-month anniversary' beside it.

'Four weeks!' she yelled. 'That's how long I've got!'

'Well... how about just a bowl of cereal then?' goes Mum.

Primrose took a big breath. Dennis dived under his hutch.

'Back me up, Dave,' said Mum.

Dad glanced round the room like a hare looking for a hole, but Mum had him in her headlights. There was no escape.

'There's no harm being a bit plump, Primrose,' Dad said, tentatively.

Primrose shook her mouse-nest head, opened her mouth and let out a wail. Mum put her arms round her and glared at Dad over her head, as if he'd just said something horrible.

'B-but...' goes Dad. 'If you did want to lose those few extra pounds, four weeks is plenty of time.'

A light-bulb look went over his face. 'That would be a great title for my book! "Four weeks to fitness – how to get the body you want."'

Dad said why didn't Primrose join in with me and him, test-driving his ideas?

'What have you got to lose?' he said.

'I'll do it too,' Mum offered. 'We could do it as a family.'

'We'll be Team Pinker!' goes Dad.

Primrose frowned and pursed her lips. It was the nearest we were going to get to a yes.

'That's the spirit!' said Dad. 'Now, the first thing we need is personal goals.'

'Does this mean I've got to eat?' said Primrose.

'A sensible diet and healthy exercise,' Dad said. 'Don't worry. I'll organise everything.'

Primrose grunted and sat down. Mum poured her some cereal. Dad got back to his goals. Considering one of his favourite mottoes is 'Never do today what you can put off till tomorrow,' he seemed surprisingly keen to get started.

He stuck a gold smiley on the space at the top of the family organiser and asked me what my goal was.

'Well, I want to be super-fit like Toby,' I said.

Dad wrote,

I will be super-fit like Toby

next to my smiley.

He stuck a red smiley underneath my gold one and wrote,

I will fit into that dress

Next to his own sticker he wrote,

I will lose one stone

Mum asked him why he wanted to lose a stone and he said his coach on the Thursday League football team had been on at him before Christmas to lose the paunch or he'd be on the bench.

He stuck one of Mum's green stickers under the others.

'I will... join in?' suggested Mum.

Once all our personal goals were on the Family Organiser, Dad said he and Primrose should have a weigh-in, so they could see how much they had lost by the end of the four weeks. Mum and me didn't want to lose weight, but we weighed in too, to keep them company.

Dad wrote our weights on the family organiser beside our goals. Of course, we all knew it was a game really. Stickers and goals and weigh-ins were easy. There was no way Dad was ever going to follow through with the difficult bit and actually work out a fitness-plan.

As he likes to say, 'When the going gets tough, there's always TV!'

Chapter 4
Who are you and what have you done with my dad?

That afternoon, Dad had to go to a football match, it being Sunday and everything, and when he got home he had to write his report.

The next day he was at the office. Everyone at the Three Towns Gazette goes in on Mondays because the paper goes to press first thing on

Tuesday. It looked as if Dad's book about getting fit in four weeks was going the way his plans always went: that is, nowhere fast.

Mum was bored because she didn't have any gardening jobs to do.

'Sitting around here is as exciting watching slugs hibernate,' she said.

Do slugs hibernate? Jess would know. If they do, they couldn't choose a more peaceful spot than Polgotherick in the winter. Half the shops are closed up, the holiday homes are empty and all the visitors have gone.

Primrose was in a state because Matt said he couldn't come over. He told her he had some kind of family thing on, but she was convinced that was just an excuse. The truth was he must have noticed she was turning into a lardy lump and he didn't want to go out with her any more.

'If he wants to break off with me, he should have the guts to say so!' she said.

'I'm sure if he did want to break off with you, he would,' said Mum. 'Now, why don't we three girls have a lovely day out?'

Mum's idea of a lovely day out is a drive over to the massive garden centre at Crewham Cross to look at the plants. This is actually not quite as bad as it sounds. For a start, there's a cafe with the best ever apple pie and ice cream, and then there's the pets' corner, where you can pick up the rabbits and guinea pigs.

Primrose isn't interested in apple pie and guinea pigs but she does like boys, and there always seem to be quite a few of them at Crewham Cross, shifting bags of compost and helping people load up their cars.

'Oh, all right,' she said. 'Why not? It isn't as if there's anything else to do.'

By the time Primrose had tried on everything in her wardrobe, done her hair and got made up like a model, Mum and me had had our lunch. Primrose didn't want any lunch, which meant she got a lecture all the way up the zig-zag path. There aren't any roads in this part of Polgotherick because the houses were built before cars were invented. You have to park on the top road and walk down.

'Nobody really looks like those models in magazines,' Mum said. 'The pictures are digitally altered. If they really had legs that long and thin they wouldn't be able to stand up on them!'

'Whatever,' muttered Primrose.

You can't let Primrose being a pain and Mum trying to be super-reasonable stop you having a nice time, because if you did you'd be as miserable as a duck in the desert, so I put my earphones in and turned up my iPod till we got there, and then

I made straight for the pets' corner.

Mum said we should meet in the cafe for tea at four o'clock, which we did, but then Primrose didn't want any apple pie and Mum had another go, so to be honest by the time we got home, all that trying to have a nice time had worn me down.

Primrose stomped straight up to her room. I sat on the rug with Dennis. Mum opened the fridge to start making supper. She let out a shriek. All the food had gone and the fridge was crammed full of cardboard boxes.

'Dave!' she screamed up the stairs. 'What's all this stuff in the fridge?'

Dad came down from his study. He looked very pleased with himself.

'I managed to get to the cash-and-carry on my way home. First part of Mission Fitness accomplished – healthy food!'

Mum pulled one of the boxes. She held it between her thumb and two fingers, as if she didn't really want to touch it.

'Eat-lite ready-meal for one,' she read.

'The rest are in the freezer,' said Dad. 'I've bought enough for everyone for the whole four weeks.'

Mum opened her mouth to say something but nothing came out. Dad thought she was speechless with admiration. He flung open the food cupboard. It was choc-a-bloc with boxes too.

'Slimsnax,' he announced, proudly. 'In case we get peckish between meals!'

Mum gave me a look that said, 'Who is this stranger in our house and what has he done with your dad?'

I shrugged and shook my head. Search me!

'I can see you're impressed,' said Dad. 'None of you believed me when I said I would work out a fitness plan, but I have!'

Dad said you had to understand how much he wanted to write his book. He had never wanted anything so much before. This was his big chance and he was not going to mess it up

Mum finally found her voice. It came out unusually quiet.

'Where is all the proper food?'

Dad was taken aback.

'This *is* proper food,' he said. 'It's got all the nutrients you need but half the calories. I dumped the old stuff in the dustbin.'

Mum took a slow breath.

'How much did this lot set you back?'

'Well, it was a bit expensive... but it's only for four weeks, isn't it? And it'll be worth it when we all end up leaner and fitter.'

I picked up Dennis and went to get a closer look.

The pictures on the boxes looked a squillion times tastier than some of the meals Mum makes, and there was no sign of any of her favourite vegetables such as parsnips, cabbage and beetroot.

'You just pop these in the microwave and hey presto, perfect dinners every time,' said Dad. 'How about that, Jan? A whole month off from cooking.'

'I like cooking,' said Mum.

Mum said she needed some air. She opened the back door and went outside. We could see her through the glass, walking round and round the yard like a prisoner plotting a break-out.

By the time she came indoors again her voice had gone back to normal. She said it had just been a surprise, seeing her fridge full of ready-meals, but she was one hundred per cent behind Dad with writing his book, and she would support him in testing out his ideas.

'I'm sure you've done a lot of research about calories and so on,' she said, not sounding very sure at all.

'Of course,' said Dad, not sounding very convincing.

Mum managed to stay positive even when we microwaved four fish-bake dinners and put them out on the plates. Each one was a tiny bit of fish under a thin lid of yellowish mashed potato, with three green beans and a few slices of carrot.

On the upside, it was the first time in ages that Primrose ate all her dinner, so at least we didn't end up with the usual huge row. On the downside, I was nearly as hungry when I finished as I had been before I sat down.

Mr Kaminski popped in like he often does around tea-time. Usually, Mum says, 'Come in, Mr K, there's plenty to go round!' This time she said, 'We're just about to have our Eat-lite puddings – would you like me to pop one in the microwave for you?'

She opened the fridge door to show him all the boxes. Mr Kaminski looked perplexed. Even when Dad explained about the fitness thing, he still didn't understand. He said you needed proper food if you wanted to get fit. He squinted at the side of the boxes, trying to read the ingredients.

'Mono-diglicerides... what is? Rusk... what for you need rusk in fish bake?'

'It's only for four weeks,' said Mum.

Mr Kaminski shook his head in a you-must-be-crazy kind of way, but he still accepted an Eat-lite Choc Delight, which looked like a scrummy gooey chocolate pudding on the box but turned out to be a dried-up sponge in a tiny pot with no goo in the middle at all.

Dad said there were two parts in his fitness plan – a calorie-controlled diet and daily exercise.

The best exercise was a brisk jog before breakfast, and he'd worked out a route for us all that would involve plenty of hills. Mum pointed out that it would be impossible to find a route in Polgotherick that didn't involve plenty of hills, but he let that go.

'Why does it have to be before breakfast?' asked Primrose, who isn't really at her best until the afternoon. Mum says she's just like Dad. His morning motto is, 'The early bird wishes he was still in bed.'

Dad said if we left it till later in the day we wouldn't do it.

'Does it have to be jogging?' said Mum. 'I don't really like jogging.'

Dad said we didn't have to like it – we just had to do it. 'No pain, no gain,' he said. It was the kind of thing that Toby's dad might say and not sound weird.

'But tomorrow's the first day of term,' said Primrose.

'Tomorrow's the first day of our four weeks,' said Dad, pointing to the family organiser. 'Look – in exactly four weeks minus one day it's your anniversary. You want to fit into that dress, don't you? PMA, Primrose!'

Mum said a Positive Mental Attitude was all very well, but she was the one who would have to get Primrose up a whole hour earlier than usual, and it was bad enough trying to prise her out of bed at the normal time on a school day.

Dad reminded her that her goal was, 'I will join in.' We were a team now. We were Team Pinker.

'I'll get up first and make sure everyone's awake,' he said. We all blinked at him.

Mr Kaminski's tummy rumbled like a train in a tunnel and he got up to go. He was probably going to get some cheese on toast or sausage and mash for his tea. The thought of it nearly made me dribble.

When he had gone I pointed out that me and Mum didn't want to lose weight – we just wanted to get fit. So maybe we should just do the jogging and not the Eat-lite dinners and Slimsnax bars.

Dad looked a bit disappointed. He said these meals were scientific and they had all the nutrients you needed, and he really felt me and Mum could manage a few weeks sticking to the rules to support him and Primrose.

We didn't have much choice anyway because he'd thrown all the normal food away. When Matt came round after supper we turned out the cupboards looking for a biscuit or packet of crisps to give him and we couldn't find anything except Slimsnax, which he didn't like the look of.

'What's brought all this on?' he asked.

'Dad's writing a book called "Four weeks to fitness",' Primrose told him. 'We're his guinea pigs, helping him test his ideas out.' She didn't want him to know that she could hardly do her famous first-date dress up any more.

Matt said he hoped Primrose could stop the diet one day early because after their walk on the coast path, he wanted to take her out for a meal at the Happy Haddock to celebrate the best six months of his whole entire life.

Everyone else went upstairs and I sat down on the rug with Dennis again. I was just wondering what his chew sticks tasted like when Matt sneaked back down. He took a little black velvet box out of his pocket. Listening to check no-one was coming, he opened it and showed me what was inside. It was a silver heart on a delicate chain.

'It's for our anniversary,' he said. 'What do you think? Will Primrose like it?'

I thought, *O-ooooooh, dear*.

He was so excited. He had absolutely no idea what was going to happen if Primrose couldn't fit into that dress. She would dump him for certain sure. That's what she was like. There was no problem so small she couldn't blow it up into a massive ginormous crisis.

'I think she'll love it,' I said.

Chapter 5
The first one awake and Fitness Flakes

If you go to bed hungry you wake up feeling like you could eat your pillow – fact. On the upside, it was half past six and there was no way anyone else would actually be up, even if they had set their alarms like we agreed.

My plan was to sneak downstairs and grab a handful of Slimsnax bars to keep me going till breakfast. They tasted like sawdust and didn't fill you up – I knew that because I'd had one for my

44

bedtime snack – but they were supposed to be nutritious and we did have a cupboard full of them.

I put my dressing gown on and tiptoed to the door. I was just about to open it when rat-a-tat-tat! Someone knocked and made me jump nearly out of my skin. I wasn't the first one awake.

'Rise and shine, Sleepy-head!'

It was Dad! I heard him knock on Primrose's door too. Knock... groan. Knock, knock... groan. Knock, knock, knock...

'Go away, Dad!'

'I thought you wanted to fit into that dress,' said Dad.

Five minutes later we were all assembled by the front door. Dad was jogging on the spot in his footie shorts. Mum was fumbling with her trainers, trying to do them up with her eyes shut. I had dug out my PE kit and Primrose was wearing last year's beach shorts and pink canvas shoes.

Anyone who saw us taking off down the front steps would have thought we were a raggle-taggle bunch, but nobody was likely to see us because a) it was still dark except for the street lights and b) anyone with a scrap of sense would be tucked up warm in bed.

Dad's route took us downhill towards the harbour first, which was just as well considering we were still half-asleep. Primrose trailed at the back, complaining about the cold. She said her toes were like icicles. They would probably snap off and rattle around in her shoes, and it would be all Dad's fault.

'Think about your goal, Primrose,' he said, not looking back. 'Keep running towards your goal. "I will fit into that dress!"'

Primrose mumbled and grumbled. A fat lot of good it would do her to fit into that dress if she died trying, she said. People could freeze to death, you know. People could get exhaustion and just keel over.

'I will fit into that dress!' said Dad, over his shoulder. 'I will fit into that dress!'

We came to the corner by the Reading Room. The bench under the street light would have looked quite tempting if it hadn't been covered in frost. Primrose sat down on it anyway.

'This is stupid,' she gasped. Her breath billowed out in clouds. 'I'm going back.'

Mum coaxed her up onto her feet again and linked arms with her. We all trudged on down the zig-zag path.

'I will fit into that dress!' cried Dad. 'I will... Oh!'

He nearly bumped into Miss Mullen as she came out of the bakery with a tray of warm bread rolls. Her eyebrows jumped like jelly-beans under her baker's bonnet.

'Good morning, Miss Mullen,' said Mum, managing to keep a straight face, as we all ran by.

We turned the corner and collapsed into giggles in the doorway of Harbour Crafts.

Mum said, 'I will fit into that dress!'

Dad said, 'It isn't funny.'

Primrose said, 'Yes it is!'

I wondered what other people would find the most surprising – all the Pinkers running around in the dead of the night or Dad shouting, 'I will fit into that dress!'

Lights were starting to come on in the houses around the harbour. Their reflections shimmered and shifted in the black water. We followed Dad up the steps on the far side of the harbour that come out onto School Lane. It actually isn't a lane at all, but a narrow path winding up to the bottom of Thistle Hill.

By the time we got to the coastal path we were all so puffed out, we weren't so much jogging as trudging.

I thought for a horrible minute that Dad was going to take us out of Polgotherick along the cliffs, but we cut back towards the town and took the most direct route back to our house.

By the time we got home we were starving. Dad was bright red and covered in sweat. It took him about five hours to stop gasping. Mum wasn't too bad, but then she works outdoors digging and stuff all day long, so she's used to it.

'What's for breakfast?' Primrose said, which, considering she usually makes such a big thing of not eating breakfast, came as a bit of a surprise. Mum looked delighted.

Dad produced a box of Fitness Flakes and a bottle of red-top milk. In case you're wondering, Fitness Flakes are like scraps of cardboard but not quite as tasty, and red-top milk is skimmed, which means it's basically water and doesn't taste of anything at all.

It was our first fit-in-four-weeks breakfast. The Fitness Flakes took a lot of chewing and, while we were chomping our way through them, Dad said he was very proud of his team. He put a tick on the family organiser to show we had all done our exercise that day.

Just when I was thinking, 'He'll never keep this up,' he announced that now we knew our route he was going to be doing a longer run. He had planned it out and would be leaving a bit before us every day so he could get back at the same time.

'Right!' he said, jumping up and dumping his empty bowl in the sink. 'I'm going to go and write some notes for my chapter on exercise.'

He took the stairs two at a time. I couldn't remember ever seeing him do that before.

'Is it just me or is Dad acting really weird?' Primrose said as we walked up the hill after breakfast. 'It's like he's changed into a football coach or something.'

We agreed that it couldn't last but in the meantime we might as well go along with it. She wanted to get thin, I wanted to get fit, and like he said, sports and fitness was his specialist subject, even if up to now it had mostly been watching other people get fit and play sports.

When I got to school, I asked Toby if he had anything edible in his back-pack – he always carries emergency supplies. He produced a thick slab of Kendal Mint Cake, which is so sweet you can almost feel it dissolving your teeth. I didn't care. I ate the whole lot.

All I could think about all morning was dinner, and buying a big double helping of chips.

Chapter 6
Girls together and the ghost at the window

The next morning, I fell out of bed when my alarm went off and fumbled out onto the landing in search of Slimsnax, only to bump straight into Mum. She told me Dad had already left for his run and therefore, just like she had said would happen, she was the one who would have to get Primrose out of bed.

'Dad's already gone?' I mumbled. 'Are you sure? It's half past six!'

'Go up and look for yourself if you like,' said Mum.

I went up to their room. The houses in Harbour Row are very tall and thin. There's the kitchen on the ground floor, the living room above that, mine and Primrose's bedrooms up the next flight of stairs, and Mum and Dad's room at the top. Their bed was empty. I checked the ensuite and Dad's study. He wasn't there.

By the time I got back down the stairs to our landing, Primrose was getting dressed and Mum had gone on down to the kitchen to find her trainers.

'Actually, this is nice, isn't it?' she said, as we set off down the front steps. 'Girls together!'

On the upside, the weather wasn't so cold; on the downside, it was murky and damp with a fine drip of drizzle. Primrose was full-on complaining she was wet through before we had even got to the end of the terrace.

When Primrose gets whiny, Mum goes into cheery overdrive, and quite honestly I don't know which is worse.

'It's only a bit of mist,' she cried. 'It makes the town look splendidly spooky, doesn't it? It's like a murder mystery film.'

'My hair's frizzing up – I can feel it!' Primrose grumbled. 'I've got water running down my back.'

'Don't let's waste our energy chatting,' Mum said. 'Onwards and upwards!'

The mist swirled round the street lamps and lurked in the doorways. It covered our clothes in tiny droplets and made our lips taste salty.

Primrose stopped grumbling, and started puffing and panting like someone going for gold in the Olympic Puffing and Panting event. She kept it up all the way down to the harbour. When we hit the steps up to School Lane she suddenly stopped dead and bent double, clutching her chest.

'I'm having a heart attack!' she cried.

Mum stopped and turned round. She rolled her eyes and started walking back.

'You are fifteen years old. I don't think your heart should be quite worn out just yet.'

Primrose said her heart was beating so hard she couldn't breathe. It felt like it was trying to dislodge itself. What if it came clean away and dropped into her stomach?

Mum said she didn't think that was likely to happen, but if it did it would be better if we'd managed to get as far as Thistle Hill because that's where Dr Murphy lived.

Primrose stood up, droopily. She put on her

most tragic, brave, suffering face. She let Mum coax her up the steps.

I don't know about Primrose's heart but all this waiting around was making my stomach feel like it was starting to digest itself. I ran on ahead, up School Lane and Thistle Hill and all the way back to our house.

When I got there I stopped to catch my breath at the bottom of the steps. The lights were on in our house but the mist made everything milky, like I was looking through tracing paper.

I glanced up at Mr Kaminski's unlit window. A pale figure goggled at me like a ghost, and then melted away in the blackness.

It freaked me out. I legged it up the front steps and burst indoors.

'A sprint finish,' goes Dad. 'Impressive!'

As soon as I was inside I felt a bit silly for getting spooked like that. Probably, if you got really, really hungry you started seeing things. Yes – that would be it.

I flopped down on the chair next to Dad and he poured some skimmed milk over my Fitness Flakes.

For someone who had got up at six o'clock and run twice as far as we had, he didn't look too bad. His face was glistening with sweat and his shirt had a damp patch all down the front; he had a towel round his neck and his socks were wet, but he didn't seem very tired.

I was still trying to chew through my first mouthful of Fitness Flakes when Mum and Primrose arrived.

'Didn't Primrose do well?' Mum said to Dad. 'It was a struggle, but she made it!'

Ahem! Excuse me – younger sister here, who did even better!

'You shouldn't have gone running off like that,' Mum said to me. 'What were you thinking?' She actually wagged her finger. 'You are far too young to be out in this fog on your own.'

See, that's the other thing that happens when Primrose gets whiny – Mum manages not to explode at her, but then gets tetchy with me! It was annoying, and I was still annoyed by the time I got to school. I stayed annoyed all day and I didn't feel like going straight home afterwards.

I texted Mum to tell her I was going to the Happy Haddock to see Gran after school. When I got there, Magnus was lying across the doorway, fast asleep. You could hear his snores half way round the harbour. He wasn't going anywhere so I had to step over him, which wasn't easy, what with him being so bulky. I had to do more of a jump.

The net of twinkly lights on the ceiling was lit up as usual because the windows were so small and the walls were so thick that hardly any daylight could get in. I spotted Jane in the gloom at the far side of the room, reading her Three Towns Gazette. She smiled and said hello.

I went on up to Gran's room. She had popped out to the baker's for a bag of yum-yums when I told her I was coming, and she had just opened a bottle of my favourite raspberry-and-apple.

We sat at the little round table in front of her window, watching the boats bobbing on the water, and I told her everything that had happened since New Year – the walk to Pike's Bluff, and wanting to get fit, and Primrose's problems with her anniversary dress.

I told her about Dad's fit-in-four-weeks plan, the Eat-lite dinners and Slimsnax bars and early-morning jogging. She said Mr K had already given her the gist. He wasn't very taken with his Eat-lite chocolate pud!

'The thing is, Dad's acting really weird,' I said. 'He's getting up early and doing runs and organising all our food and stuff. I mean, you know what he's usually like.'

Gran nodded. She got that faraway smile she sometimes gets when she thinks about Dad, as if she can see right back across the years to when he was a little boy.

'Well, you know,' she said, 'I have once seen him get all fired up like this before. It was when he first met your mum and he was desperate for her to fall in love with him.'

Gran said perhaps Dad was a slow-burn kind of person – it took him about fifteen years to work himself up to something, but when he did, he went all out. He must really, really, really want to write that book, she said.

Gran offered me the last yum-yum. She said Dad probably did know his stuff but he was writing a book for grown-ups. He might not have thought about how it might be a bit different for children. I was still growing, and when you're still growing you need plenty of good food to fill you up.

Suddenly there was a volley of barks and snarls from downstairs. Someone who wasn't very good at long jump must have tried to get past Magnus.

Gran said, 'Let's have a little walk!'

Jane was behind the bar pouring some beer for a customer and Magnus was glaring at him as if he would like to take a bite out of his leg. Outside, it was already starting to get dark.

Gran marched purposefully into Harbourside Stores. She always does her shopping there. Her mum used to send her down there with a list when she was a little girl and she says some of the wooden shelves on the end wall are still the very same.

She bought a box of berry oatcakes and stuffed it in the top of my school-bag.

'Emergency supplies,' she said, 'just in case you need a little top-up.'

Chapter 7
The proof of the pudding and Toby's tepee

One whole week later, I still hadn't opened that pack of berry oatcakes. I didn't want to cheat, since it mattered so much to Dad. I felt quite proud of myself because berry oatcakes aren't as bad as they sound and it's very hard to resist a tasty treat when you're faced with a jog before breakfast.

It was misty most mornings that week, and I wished Mum would stop saying it reminded her of murder mysteries. When Primrose kept complaining and coming over faint, stopping and starting, going slowly and then slowing down a bit more, I could cheerfully have dragged her into a dark alley and throttled her.

It was tough living on Eat-lite ready-meals, sawdust Slimsnax and cardboard Fitness Flakes and it was even tougher trailing round Polgotherick in the dismal dark with Primrose being a pain and Mum being patient, but it was worth it because Dad was delighted.

He put his big ticks on the family organiser every day to show we had stuck to the diet and done our exercise, and he always bounced off upstairs after breakfast to work on his book.

Amazingly, he also got up before the rest of us and ran further every morning, and by the time we got home he had breakfast on the table. He looked as fresh as a daisy, though a bit sweaty. As fresh as a dewy daisy!

When Mum remarked on the difference between Day One, when we all ran together and he staggered back looking as if he was going to die, and how great he looked in the mornings now, he said that was the proof of the pudding. His fitness plan was already making him fitter.

The mention of pudding didn't help the Fitness Flakes and skimmed milk go down, but it did give me a happy flash-forward to dinner-time. I had stopped doubling up on chips and started having two puddings instead. After what Gran said about me still growing and everything, it seemed OK to eat what I wanted outside the house, so long as I was managing to stick to Dad's diet at home.

At the beginning of Week Two, Toby invited me and Jess round after school for tea in his tepee. I was twice-over keen. For one thing, I couldn't wait to see what a real live tepee looked like, and for another thing, it meant proper food instead of Eat-lite Chicken Delight.

Jess had never been to Toby's house before, but she reckoned after the walk to Pike's Bluff she knew what to expect. Ha ha! It was quite funny seeing her face when she realised we had to put the tepee up ourselves, with Toby's mum not helping and his dad still at work.

'Self-sufficiency!' Toby's mum and dad say, when they make Toby and Leah do things themselves.

'Right,' Toby said, reading the instructions. 'We take this bit of fabric and put it on the ground where the pole's going to be...'

It was a square of material with some lines going from the centre to the corners and edges. We put it in the middle of the lawn.

'Now we peg one end of this piece of string in the middle and use the lines on the fabric as a guide to find out where we need to put the pegs in...'

Jess and me just did what we were told. Getting the pole up was tricky and we lost Leah under five acres of canvas when it collapsed on the first try, but after about an hour of wrestling with it, we finally got it up.

'Nice job!' Toby's dad said, when he arrived home. 'I'll get the brazier.'

He brought a big metal tray on little legs out of the garage, and put it in the middle of the tepee. He got some sticks and coal and lit a fire in the brazier, opening the flap at the top of the tepee to let the smoke out.

While Toby and his dad were getting the fire going, me and Jess helped Leah and his mum to get the food. Leah wrapped some potatoes in foil to put in the edge of the flames and her mum filled a big black frying pan with sausages and burgers.

Me and Jess carried boxes of bread rolls and bananas out, and marshmallows and barbecue skewers to toast them on.

It was completely dark outside and getting chilly by the time we had got settled in. The flickering flames lit up the inside of the tepee with a warm yellow glow and soon the sausages were sizzling in the pan.

'Would you like to know five facts about tepees?' Jess asked, pulling her blanket round her. 'One: they used to be made of poles covered in buffalo skins. Two: it was the women who made them and put them up. Three: they spent the winter months decorating them with pictures of animals and things. Four: they made little tepees for play-tents for the children. Five – and this is my favourite – they made tiny tepees for dolls' houses!'

I hadn't seen Jess look so happy since her parents split up, and Toby's family were dead happy with her too. They said she was brilliant knowing all these facts, and they hoped she would be able to come to Snowdon with them.

'We'll have a few practice hikes before then,' they said, 'starting with Beacon Hill in three weeks' time.'

You could almost see Jess making a mental note to find out five facts about Beacon Hill. The only one I knew was that it was on the moor. I hadn't ever been up it.

Toby said, 'There's a tower at the top that's supposed to be haunted!'

I couldn't wait to get home and put a sticker on the family organiser. Three weeks' time was perfect – it was the last day of Dad's get-fit-in-four-weeks plan. By then, I'd be striding ahead up that hill. It would be Toby who couldn't keep up with me!

Chapter 8
The slight adjustment and the secret stash

As you might have noticed, my sister Primrose is the moodiest person on the planet, and all these early starts and starvation rations weren't exactly making her more mellow.

Matt came round every day after school as per usual, and she bit his head off at the slightest thing. When he drew a heart on the Family Organiser for their six-month anniversary she said it was the wrong colour – her stickers and everything to do with her this year had to be red.

She snapped at him when he got all mushy remembering their first date, how it all started because they were trying to help Dad to get over his fear of dogs by introducing him to Sam, the oldest, sweetest-natured dog you could ever meet.

'And your dad hid in the shed under the front steps, so we took Sam for a walk on the coast path and I promised to bring him up every day till your dad stopped being scared of him.'

'Like that was ever going to work,' said Primrose, scornfully.

'And you looked so gorgeous in that little pink dress...'

'Whatever!'

She was just as snappy when he talked about the special anniversary they were going to have.

'We'll try and get that little table in the alcove. We can have Jane's three-fish pie and raspberry meringue...'

'Don't talk about food,' said Primrose. 'You are seriously not helping.'

The snappier she got, the more Matt seemed to admire her. The fact that she was even tetchier than usual – which was quite an achievement –

just showed how tough it was for her helping Dad to test out his ideas. Yet she stuck at it. She was an angel! I wished she really was an angel because then she might flap her wings and fly away.

Unlike Matt, Mum's patience with Primrose was wearing thin. By the end of Week Two it was like an elastic band stretched to the limit, and then one morning it snapped.

Primrose was doing her I-can't-breathe-I'm-having-a-heart-attack routine when Mum suddenly stopped bending over her saying soothing things and stood up. Primrose took the gasping down a notch and looked up to see what was going on.

'We're having a slight adjustment to the way we organise our early morning runs,' Mum announced. 'From now on, I shall be running on my own. You two will have to stay together because we can't have Peony running round in the dark all by herself.'

'Why should I have to baby-sit Peony?' said Primrose. She wasn't gasping at all any more.

Like I was the one who needed baby-sitting!

'Why do I have to be stuck with Primrose and you get to run at your own speed?' I said. 'I want to run with you.'

But Mum declared she was sure we would both be fine and then she just took off. I didn't really blame her. Everyone sometimes reaches a point with Primrose when they have to get away quick before they completely lose their rag.

As it turned out, running with just Primrose was slightly less of a pain because she didn't bother with the gasping, collapsing and clutching her chest thing. She knew it was a waste of time trying to get sympathy from me. She just flopped and trudged and grumbled along, which was slow but at least it was steady.

The second time we had to run on our own, Primrose more or less ignored me, but the third day, she was spoiling for a fight.

'You trod on my heel, you little rat-bag. Back off!' she yelled, clutching her foot.

'I wasn't anywhere near you!'

'Yes you were. Look!' She flashed her heel at me. It looked completely normal.

'Go away,' said Primrose.

'I wish I could.'

'Well you can. I'm in charge and I say you'll be all right on your own.'

'Mum said we have to stay together,' I said.

'Mum isn't here.'

Considering Primrose's top speed so far had been about Dad's normal ambling pace plus stops, she shot off at a surprising speed. She disappeared round the bottom corner and by the time I came out at the harbour she was nowhere to be seen.

What was I supposed to do now? If I went home, Dad would be disappointed I hadn't done my jog. If I did my jog, Mum would be cross that I ran on my own. I was stuck unless I managed to find Primrose, but if I did manage to find her, I'd have to put up with her.

I walked slowly all the way along the harbour, pondering what to do. Then I walked back again. The stars were fading in the cold, clear sky, and now that I'd slowed down I was starting to shiver.

There were lights on in lots of the houses, though none of the shops were open yet, except Dot's cafe on the corner of Cave Lane. I glanced in through the steamy window as I passed... and guess who I saw?

'Primrose – you cheat!'

She was sitting there warming her hands on a steaming cup of hot chocolate.

'I came over funny,' she said. 'I thought I was going to faint.'

'What, and you just happened to be passing the cafe, and you just happened to have brought some money with you like everyone does when they go jogging?'

She planned it! She faked the argument to get rid of me so she could skive off down the cafe.

'Don't tell Mum and Dad, yeah?' she said. 'I'll buy you a hot choc too.'

It was soooo tempting! My teeth were rattling in my head, the hairs on my legs were standing up inside my jogging bottoms and my fingers were turning blue.

One moment of weakness, and I was sunk. The problem with accepting a bribe from someone is that then they've got something on you. If I told Mum and Dad that Primrose went to the cafe, she would tell them that I was there drinking hot chocolate too.

After that, we jogged straight down to Dot's cafe every day, hung around there as long as we could, then jogged back up the hill. It was much shorter than the route we were supposed to be doing, but also much faster, so I reckoned it would be just as good for my fitness.

Primrose brought enough money for us to have an egg roll with our hot choc. She said it wasn't as if she needed to lose much weight, and I wasn't trying to lose any weight at all. We weren't like Dad, trying to lose a paunch.

Primrose said we should think of the egg roll and hot choc as our breakfast. OK, we had to eat some Fitness Flakes and skimmed milk when we got home or Dad would smell a rat, but they didn't count because they didn't have anything fattening in them. Therefore we weren't really eating two breakfasts at all.

I wasn't sure about that, and I also wasn't sure she was right that the stress of getting up so early was enough to make us thin.

'You can feel the kilos dropping off with all that struggling to get out of bed,' she said.

All I knew was, I was doing a bit more exercise than usual and, like Gran says, every little helps. If I could jog up and down to the harbour then surely walking up Beacon Hill should be a piece of cake.

I managed not to feel guilty when Dad poured the milk on the Fitness Flakes. Like Primrose said, he was doing the exercise-and-diet thing, and that was what mattered. We were kind of supporting him, or at least, he thought we were.

Plus, he had Mum. She set off at the same time as us and arrived back a bit earlier, so she must be going at a good pace. She was usually in the shower when we got back. She was usually in a good mood too... until the morning she found the secret stash.

'Well, well, well,' she said, as she came into the kitchen. 'I was searching for some tissues in the cupboard under the phone, and look what I found.'

She had a white plastic bag in her hand. She emptied it out on the table. There was a six-pack of doughnuts with only one left, half a box of shortbread biscuits, two chocolate bars, a tin of toffees, three empty crisp packets and one bag of sweets.

'Has anyone got anything they would like to say?' asked Mum.

Chapter 9
Keep calm and don't panic!

Nobody did have anything to say. We were all too busy staring at each other accusingly. I was giving Primrose the evils because if you're caught then you ought to fess up, but she was doing a very good job of looking as astonished as I was by Mum's find.

'Oh, all right!' Dad blurted out, suddenly. 'It was me. But it's not my fault.'

'Whose fault is it, then?' asked Mum. 'The doughnut fairy's?'

'It's all very well for you to get sarky on me but what have you had to do?' said Dad. 'A bit of jogging and a holiday from cooking!'

He had decided to come out fighting, which I personally didn't think was a good idea. Mum took a long, slow breath. It seemed to blow her up to three times her normal height.

'It's not easy having to organise everything,' Dad said, sounding a bit less sure of himself. 'I've had to do all the work – making the fitness plan, buying the food, planning the running routes. And I've had to keep everyone up to the mark.'

'Everyone except yourself,' said Mum.

Dad was starting to crumble.

'I've had the book to write as well,' he whined. 'Writing a book is a lot more stressful than you think!'

'And that's your excuse, is it?' said Mum.

Dad said there was no excuse. He had let us down. He looked as crestfallen as a cockerel who's lost his hens. He doesn't usually do crestfallen, so we were all a bit taken aback.

It was Mum's turn to crumble then. She said actually, maybe it was understandable. Lots of people started comfort eating when they were under pressure and she hadn't really thought about all the stress this fitness business must be putting on Dad.

'When you come to think about it, handling stress is part of fitness too,' she said. 'We could do some stress-busting things so you don't have to comfort-eat any more, and then you could write a chapter about it in your book.'

'But I don't know any stress-busting things,' Dad said. 'I thought I just had to do diet and exercise. This is terrible!'

Mum tried to back-track since the subject of stress seemed to be stressing Dad out, but it was no good. She said she would find out about stress-busting stuff for him. She would make the plan and keep us up to the mark, stress-wise. She would be happy to do that because she herself was feeling stressed, what with not having had any work since Christmas. People just didn't think about their gardens in January.

'Normally, I cook if I get stressed,' she said. 'So it'll be good for me to find something else to do, for the time being.'

Aah... Mum's cooking. I could almost taste her sautéed sprouts and apricot fritters just thinking about it. I was surprised to find I was really missing it.

'Do we have to do stress-busting too? Primrose asked. 'Only, some of us aren't comfort eating, plus we've got other things to keep us busy such as, for example, having a life.'

Mum said we were Team Pinker and that meant everyone sticking to the plan.

'Except Dad,' Primrose mumbled.

At such moments, what you want is a distraction, and hey presto, Mum's friend Stella arrived. She's as lean and lively as a greyhound, although she's even older than Mum and has a white badger-stripe down her parting.

'Great news!' she boomed. 'Garden Angels has got a job!'

Mum jumped up and grabbed the green pen to write on the family organiser.

'It's next weekend,' Jane said. 'We're digging a pond for the pink house on Acre Lane.'

There wasn't much room to write on next weekend. Mum had to squeeze in 'pink house pond' between Primrose's anniversary and my morning at the kennels on the Saturday, and my walk up Beacon Hill and the big weigh-in on the Sunday.

'Gosh!' Stella exclaimed, suddenly noticing the snack stash tipped out on the table. 'I thought you still had another week to go with the diet.'

Dad looked sheepish. Mum covered for him.

'These are visual aids, to remind us about all

the things we mustn't eat between meals,' she said, stuffing them back into the carrier bag.

Primrose rolled her eyes, and Stella looked at her quizzically. Mum said, 'We were just talking about stress.'

'I know all about that,' said Stella. 'I've been practising yoga for twenty years. Would you like me to show you some stress-busting exercises?'

Dad perked up and got all keen again. He never stays gloomy very long. He can't be bothered!

Stella got us all to lie down on the floor. Dennis was delighted. He jumped down from his lookout on the roof of his hutch and hopped round us, sniffing our hair and bouncing over our legs. Stella said she wasn't used to having animals joining in with yoga exercises but we all agreed that Dennis's huffing and hopping was actually rather restful.

Stella said all the yoga exercises had names and this one was called the corpse pose. Basically, we had to shut our eyes and act dead, except for breathing steadily in and out, which obviously real corpses don't do. They don't snore either, so Dad wasn't getting it quite right when, five minutes later, Gran called in.

It isn't every day your gran walks in to find the whole family lined up on the kitchen floor like sausages under the grill. Mum sat up and explained what we were doing. She gave Dad a hefty nudge. He spluttered back to life.

'Well don't mind me if you want to go on with your... er... exercises,' Gran said. 'I just came to tell you the removals men are booked, and I'll be moving into Nash House at the weekend.'

She stepped carefully over us to get to the family organiser, pen at the ready.

'Ooh – it looks like you've got rather a lot on! I'll put it in the margin with an arrow.'

By that time we were all on our feet except Dennis, who was doing a rabbit version of the corpse pose in his favourite spot under the radiator.

'Would you like to try a balance pose now?' Stella said. 'They're very good for de-stressing.'

Gran said she could do with a bit of de-stressing after walking in on so many family corpses, so she joined in. We did something called the tree pose, which meant we had to try and stand on one leg and put our hands together above our heads, although I thought we'd have looked more like a tree with both feet on the ground and our arms spread out.

Dad's tree kept pitching over to one side as if it was getting hit by gusts of wind, and then toppling over. That made everybody laugh.

'It isn't working,' Dad said.

'Yes, it is,' said Stella. 'Laughing is a great de-stresser too.'

Dad was delighted with Stella. He got his notebook and took down lots of ideas for his chapter on stress.

'I'm going to call it "Keep calm and don't panic,"' he said. 'I'll start straight away, while it's fresh.'

He turned on his laptop and sat tippety-tapping at the keys while Mum made tea for Gran and Stella. I sat down with Dennis and he hopped up onto my lap for a cuddle.

It was as calm in the kitchen as when we were all playing dead. Then suddenly Dad stopped tippety-tapping. He thumped a few keys. He gave his laptop a shake.

'Well isn't that just great?' he cried. 'Isn't this just fine and dandy? My blooming computer's crashed!'

It was always love-hate between Dad and his laptop. He thought it played up just to annoy him.

'Why are you doing this?' he yelled at it. 'Stop right now or I'll have you recycled. I mean it!'

Mum said it was the perfect opportunity for him to keep calm and not panic, but to be honest that really didn't help things at all.

Chapter 10
The whale and the goldfish

Dad's laptop went on playing up for days. He said it was only Stella's stress-busting exercises that got him through it.

'Well, and Matt,' said Mum.

It was a fair point, considering that Matt took one look at it and fixed it when he walked in after school on Thursday to find Dad threatening to throw it out the window. Dad said on the upside, it was fixed, but on the downside it took a teenage boy to fix it. Then he did some tree poses.

That evening, Dad came home from five-a-side and did some more tree poses. The coach had made him sit out for the whole session.

'He put me on the bench,' said Dad, rocking from side to side on one leg. 'He actually said, "Don't break it!"'

Mum was outraged. 'You might have put on a little bit of weight with all that comfort eating,' she said, 'but you must still be pretty fit. You've been jogging for miles every morning.'

Dad tried to stretch his arms in the air and toppled over as if he'd been felled by an invisible lumberjack. After a few more tries, he gave up and watched some Simpsons. Stella did say that laughing was good for stress-busting too.

On Friday, Primrose and me did our usual early morning dive into Dot's Cafe. There was something delicious about sitting inside eating egg and bacon rolls when we were supposed to be running around in the dark.

Primrose was in a good mood. She seemed to like these secret breakfasts as much as I did, once she'd got over the trauma of having to get out of bed early.

'So tomorrow's the big day,' I said. 'Have you tried on your dress?'

She shook her head.

'No, but it's bound to fit better now, isn't it? I mean, we're getting up at the crack of dawn, jogging down here and doing yoga stuff, and it was only a little bit too tight.'

A little bit too tight? As in, skunks are a little bit too smelly?

'We have been eating two breakfasts,' I pointed out.

'Yes, but Fitness Flakes don't count,' goes Primrose. 'It isn't as if we've been filling our faces with doughnuts all day like Dad.'

'No-o...' I tried not to think about my new nickname at school, Two-puddings Peony.

Primrose doesn't usually talk about anything but herself but, like I said, she was in a good mood. She asked me what the plan was for Sunday, and our walk up Beacon Hill. She even seemed quite interested when I told her. Talking about it made me feel more excited than ever. Just one more day to get through and then Hello Sunday, and Eat my dust, Super-fit-Toby!

But as it turned out, that Saturday was a lo-o-o-o-o-ong day. We didn't do our jog on Saturdays because I already had to get up really early to work at the kennels and Primrose couldn't cope without at least one proper lie-in every week.

Normally, when I get up, everyone else is still in bed. Mum sometimes pops down to say cheerio and have a nice morning, but I don't mind if she doesn't. That morning when I went downstairs, Mum was already up. She said she was far too keen to get going to lie around in bed.

'It's our first proper gardening job since Christmas,' she said. 'There's nothing like getting stuck in to some good heavy clearing and digging!'

She was like Jamie Grey in Year 5's little brother when he's been at the Smarties, running around and talking too much.

'Where did I put my gardening gloves? What's wrong with this back door key? I hope Stella's bringing a flask. I'd better call her! Where's my mobile?...'

I felt cheated out of my peace and quiet because I really like the feeling of being the only one awake. I like creeping around and shutting the front door quietly after me.

Crash! Mum managed to get the back door open. 'Hello Stella!' She got through on her mobile just as the door hit the wall. She went out into the yard to look for her gardening gloves, talking at the top of her voice.

I waved out the window and went. As I walked up the zig-zag path, the lights were coming on in the houses. My friend Becky was waiting for me outside her house and we took the footpath across the field to Hayden's Lane.

Becky's older than me, but she's lovely to talk to. She really listens, unlike some people I could mention. She totally understood why I was annoyed with Mum, and she totally remembered all the things we had on the family organiser that weekend.

As we cleaned out the pens and walked the dogs around the three meadows, we chatted about Primrose and Matt. Becky knows Matt because his family own the kennels, but that's a whole nother story. ("How to get what you want by Peony Pinker," to be precise.) Then we talked about Beacon Hill and the weigh-in, and Dad's secret stash, and Mum's pond-digging.

It was a sunny morning but quite chilly, so we couldn't hang around. We got through all our jobs by twelve o'clock and went back to Becky's house for a sandwich.

When I got home, Primrose pounced on me.

'Mum and Dad are out — you've got to help me!' she said.

She had done her make-up and pinned her hair with a pink fabric flower, and she was wearing the anniversary dress. It actually looked quite loose, but when she turned her back to me, I saw why.

'Can you do my zip up?'

I could see it wasn't going to work but I pretended to try. I tugged at the zip.

'Come on, Peony. Hurry up,' goes Primrose. 'What's the problem?'

'It seems to be stuck,' I said.

She pulled away and went to the mirror, twisting round to see the back of her dress. She let out a shriek.

'I'm a whale!' she blubbed. 'What's happened to me?'

Two breakfasts every day for a month, that's what's happened, I thought.

'Wear your coat on top,' I suggested. 'He'll never notice.'

Primrose told me I was being ridiculous, which was a bit rich in the circumstances.

'I can't go,' she said. 'I was really looking forward to it and I can't go.'

Then she flopped on the floor and sat there looking droopy, like Cinderella waiting for her fairy godmother to come and say, 'You shall go to the ball!'

Unfortunately, we haven't got a fairy godmother, so after a five-minute wait, Primrose jumped up and flounced out of the room, flashing her bare back at me.

If I thought I was going to get some peace, I

was wrong, because just then our non-fairy actual mother came home for lunch.

'I'm knackered!' she announced. 'Stella's not stopping for lunch, but I said I had to come back for you girls. Make me a sandwich, Peony?'

With that, she collapsed in corpse pose on the rug. I felt like saying I was busy but I wasn't, so I found some bread and got buttering. I was slicing some cheese when there was a knock on the door. It was Matt. He looked so happy. I couldn't bear it.

Mum sat up. Matt showed her the necklace he had bought for Primrose.

'She's going to love it,' she said.

I handed Mum her sandwich and called up the stairs to Primrose. Like Gran says, it's always best to get horrible things over and done with as quick as possible, like pulling off a plaster.

'Matt's here!'

After approximately three centuries Primrose appeared in the doorway. She was like a breath of cold air. If Matt was planning to get huggy, he thought the better of it.

'Have I missed something?' Mum muttered.

Matt told Primrose she looked fantastic. 'I love you in that dress,' he said. He slipped his hand into his pocket. He was going to give her the necklace. No-o-o-o!!!

'Where's Sam?' Primrose demanded, not bothering with any of that you-look-nice stuff, though he did look nice. He was wearing the same jeans and t-shirt he wore on their first-ever date, but it's easier for boys. They always look about the same to me.

Matt pulled his hand out of his pocket and stared at Primrose like a goldfish that's hit the glass. He muttered something about Sam's arthritis playing up, and him not being able to walk very far nowadays, what with being so old and everything.

'The whole idea of our anniversary was to do the same as our first date,' said Primrose. 'Considering our first date was taking Sam for a walk on the coast path, I don't see how we can do that when you've left him at home!'

Primrose said they might as well forget about the whole thing.

'What – the anniversary or... are you dumping me?' said Matt, in disbelief.

'I think you should go,' Primrose said.

He didn't move. She made an impatient huffy noise and left the room backwards, so Matt wouldn't see her gaping zip.

Mum said, 'I'm so sorry, Matt. I don't know what's got into her. It's probably her hormones.'

After he'd gone, Mum tried to talk to Primrose

but she wouldn't open her door.

'Go away!' she said.

Mum went back to digging the pond. She had just left when Gran called in on her way up to Nash House. The removals men were bringing her furniture.

'Could you go up to the road and show them the way, Peony, while I go on ahead and open up the house?'

There's no road to Nash House. The removals men would have to park at the top of the hill and carry all Gran's beds and cupboards and stuff down the zig-zag path, then fifty metres along the coastal footpath. They were not going to be happy!

'Is Primrose already out with Matt?' said Gran.

I shook my head.

'They've had a big bust-up.'

Gran didn't look amazed. She went up to talk to Primrose. She got her to open her bedroom door. She persuaded her to put some jeans on and come and help her decide where everything should go.

As they were coming back down the stairs, I heard Gran say, 'Remember, when things hit rock bottom, the only way is up.' No-one else would ever dare say stuff like that to Primrose!

Chapter 11
Big beacons and bad lies

We borrowed the Scouts' minibus for the drive to Beacon Hill. It had enough room for Toby's parents, Toby, Leah, me, Jess and everything we would need to survive if we should accidentally take a wrong turning and end up getting lost for a month in the Arctic.

Jess, of course, knew five facts about beacons. It would never have occurred to me to look 'beacon' up. I thought it was just the name of the hill.

'A beacon is a high point with something on top to draw attention to it,' she said, as we trundled along the lanes in the creaky old bus. 'Usually, that will be a fire or light, but you can have daytime beacons such as towers or flagpoles. That's two facts.

'Number three – in the old days they used beacon fires near the sea to guide ships in – but pirates sometimes put them in the wrong places to trick ships into running aground.

'Number four – lots of hills in Britain are called Beacon Hill, and the hills between Wales and England are called the Brecon Beacons because the Welsh people used to light fires along the tops to warn everyone when the English were coming.'

'Number five – the beacon on this Beacon Hill's a ruined tower that's supposed to be haunted!'

Toby's mum said there wasn't much left of the tower but it was still worth the climb because you could see most of Cornwall from the top on a fine day. Unless a miracle happened, we weren't even going to see most of Beacon Hill, let alone Cornwall, because it was really foggy.

Toby's dad pulled into a bumpy lay-by beside a gate with a footpath sign. We all jumped out. Toby's mum did some last-minute re-organising of the back-packs so that we would all be carrying our fair share. We put on our coats and she gave us some over-trousers from the Scouts' all-weather-adventure locker behind the back seats.

'It's going to be wet walking up there today,' she said.

Toby's dad opened his waterproof map and put his compass on it, turning it this way and that like a proper explorer, although I didn't think he really needed to as the path looked like a deep ditch between high hedges and it would be nearly impossible to get lost.

But after a few hundred metres, we came to some woods and the path disappeared. We stomped along under the trees on a thick layer of pine needles and dead leaves that was as hard going as walking on sand.

Jess said she was glad she'd been doing practice walks on her own every day because this would have been pretty tough otherwise. I just hoped it would get easier once we got out of the woods.

If you think walking up a steep slope of tussocky grass and cunningly-concealed rocks just waiting for you to slip on them is easier than being ankle deep in pine needles, then I suppose it was.

'It's quite low-viz,' Toby's dad said.

'Low visibility,' Toby explained. His face was drenched in mist.

'It means we can't see very far,' said Leah. Droplets hung from her wet hair like melt-water running off icicles.

'Stick together, now,' said Toby's mum. 'We don't want anyone to get left behind.'

I was trying not to puff and pant because nobody else seemed to be having the same trouble getting enough air into their lungs. It was actually a relief when I stepped on a stone and fell over because at least it meant we stopped for a few minutes to check my ankle was all right.

'You've gone bright red!' Toby said. 'Are you OK?'

'I'm fine.'

'You probably just haven't done much wild-walking before,' said Toby's mum. 'Most people go up the easy side.'

There was an easy side?

'Let's have some Kendal Mint Cake,' suggested his dad, refolding the map.

We went a bit slower after that. We played word-games and Toby's dad told us adventure stories. I would have really enjoyed it, except it felt like someone had filled my over-trousers with earth and then topped them up with water.

It didn't help that I couldn't see more than a few metres in front of my face. I kept thinking we must be nearly at the top, we *must* be nearly at the top, but the hill just went on and on, up and up, under the thick swirling mist.

'Let's sing some songs!' said Leah.

On the upside, when they started singing no-one could hear me puffing like a hot dog, but on the downside, everyone got into the rhythm and speeded up. It was all I could do not to fall behind. So much for 'Eat my dust, Toby'! So much for Dad's fit-in-four-weeks campaign!

Suddenly, it started pouring with rain, as if someone had turned on the great cold shower in the sky. Whoosh! The rain splashed off the stones and drummed on our hoods. Toby's dad whipped out his handy all-weather shelter, which was shaped like an orange segment, and we all squashed in underneath it.

'I think it's time for lunch!' said Toby's mum.

So there we were, eating our sandwiches in the pouring rain half-way up a huge hill under an all-weather shelter with our legs sticking out... and it occurred to me that this was one of those picnics, like Hawk's Tor with the hailstones as big as marbles, or the day they rowed to the island.

It was a picnic we would always remember. We would talk about it in the future. We would say, 'That was the best picnic ever!' I forgot about my heavy legs. I tucked into my sandwiches and watched the water bouncing off my wellies and over-trousers.

Jess told us five facts about rain. Leah started a story-making game. Toby passed round wedges of cherry cake he had made himself. I would have wanted to stay there forever except I was starting to get cold, so I didn't mind when Toby's dad said, 'Who's ready to push on?'

I was ready, but my legs were not. They seemed to have gone stiff but when I struggled up to standing, they suddenly turned to jelly. As I put my back-pack on, they actually wobbled, and when I tried to set off, it was like my feet had grown roots. They would not budge.

Toby's mum said I looked very tired, which was spot on but I wasn't going to say so. If they thought I couldn't even manage Beacon Hill, what chance did I have of going up Snowdon?

So I lied.

Some lies are OK. For example, when your Gran's had a new haircut that makes her look like an electrocuted hedgehog it's all right to say you think it looks lovely. You aren't doing it to protect yourself, you're doing it to be nice.

Some lies are not OK. They are very, very bad. For example, when you're hiking up a hill with your friend Toby's super-fit family and you can't keep up because you're not fit enough but you're too proud to ask them to go slower, so you pretend you've got a tummy upset.

What happens then is that they have to abandon the whole hike and take you home, and you get upset and start to blub in the minibus but you can't tell whether that's because you've spoilt everyone else's day or because you've lied to people you like. The only thing you know for sure is that it isn't because your tummy hurts, which is what everyone else thinks.

'Never mind,' Toby's mum said. 'These things happen. We can have another practice hike when you feel better.'

'Peony and Jess could come midnight-orienteering with us,' Leah said. 'That would be good practice.'

'Yes,' agreed Toby 'and it's not until next month, so Peony's bound to be better.'

'What's orienteering?' asked Jess. Finally — something she didn't know!

'It's like a treasure trail. You have to read a map and find all the places on it,' said Toby.

'You race against lots of other teams,' said Leah.

'And do you always do it at midnight?' asked Jess.

'No, but it's much more fun in the dark!'

Toby's mum said it was a shame, practice-wise, that the particular orienteering event they were going to do wasn't hilly.

'I think you'd enjoy it though,' she said.

Considering it wasn't hilly, I thought I might enjoy it too.

Chapter 12
Cheat-snacks and sneaking

The good thing about having a sister like Primrose is that you never have to worry about being the centre of attention. When I got home, she was in a full-on flap, so there wasn't any question of anyone giving me the third degree about my tummy upset.

'It's Matt again!' she cried, shoving her phone in our faces. 'What am I going to do?'

Mum was getting the boxes out of the fridge for dinner.

'Well, you can't just keep him dangling, Primrose,' she said. 'You're going to have to answer, sooner or later.'

Dad was setting the table.

'We weren't expecting you home this early,' he said to me. 'Did you have a nice time?'

I shook my head.

'We didn't get to the top because I wasn't feeling well.'

I tried to look as if I felt sick, which I actually did when I thought about Toby and the others going down to the harbour for fish and chips while all I had to look forward to was Eat-lite shepherd's pie and strawberry dessert.

'And say what?' goes Primrose, completely ignoring me and Dad.

'I don't know,' said Mum. 'Tell him you didn't want to cancel your anniversary but just postpone it. I mean, that would make sense, wouldn't it? Your first date was at the end of July – it's the end of January now and much too cold to wear the same clothes, let alone drag poor old Sam out on the coastal path.'

'So are you saying we've got to wait until the end of a whole year?' said Primrose.

'That is a long time,' said Dad.

Primrose turned her fire on him.

'What, so you think we won't last that long?'

Mum put the first box in the microwave.

'You could do nine months – that would take you to Whitsun and it'll be much warmer by then.'

'Yes, and I'll probably be even fatter!' cried Primrose, flinging herself down on a chair.

Ping! The first dinner was done. Mum put another one in.

'Are you going to manage yours, Peony?' she asked me, as if it was a seventeen-course banquet and not a scrap of mince and potato with six soggy peas.

'If you do get fatter,' Dad said to Primrose, 'you can simply put your anniversary off again.'

'No, I can't,' said Primrose. 'Don't be silly!'

Ping! The second dinner was done.

'OK, so if you do decide to finish with him after nine months because you still can't fit into your anniversary dress...' Mum paused, trying not to roll her eyes. 'At least you'll have had three extra months of going out together!'

'And of growing up,' I mumbled, under my breath.

'What did you say?' said Primrose.

Ping!

'Could we give this a rest while we eat?' suggested Mum.

Primrose's phone rang. She glared at it.

'It's him again.'

Ping!

Mum said she was very tired. It had been a hard weekend, trying to keep up with Stella digging the pond. Stella who, by the way, was ten years older than her, which made it also plain embarrassing.

Primrose said, 'How do you think I feel?' Then she sank into a sulk like a crab in wet sand.

Dad tried to cheer everyone up by reminding us that this was our very last Eat-lite meal. As soon as we had finished, he said, we could do our weigh-in. It was exciting! We might find that we were quite a few pounds lighter. After all, the rest of us had stuck to the diet, which made him feel very proud.

He got the scales and put them in the middle of the floor. Dennis crept up to them, ready to leap back if they suddenly made a move. When they didn't, he got bold and went right up to them. He rubbed his chin on them, which is a rabbit's way of saying, 'This is mine!'

Dad's efforts at cheering us up weren't working, so he gave up and microwaved the puddings. I was just wondering what the strawberry on the top was actually made of, when Gran and Mr Kaminski called in.

'Woah!' goes Gran, taking one look at us. 'Why the long faces?'

She was in an exceptionally good mood, even for Gran, probably because she had just spent her first night in her new house. You could tell how happy she was by the way she bounced in and pulled up a chair. Mr Kaminski seemed unusually smiley too, basking in the sunshine of her cheerfulness.

'Matt keeps ringing me,' Primrose said, poutily.

'We didn't get to the top of Beacon Hill, and it was my fault,' I said.

'I'm worn out from digging that pond,' said Mum.

Dad said he was still smarting a bit from being put on the bench, but on the whole he was feeling pretty good...

Then he stood on the scales.

'This can't be right,' he muttered. He got off and stepped back on again; he was still the same weight as the first time we weighed ourselves, before we started getting fit in four weeks.

Mum was perplexed. OK, he had cheated on the diet, but those long runs every morning should have more than made up for that.

'Is not far enough, ze shed,' said Mr Kaminski.

'The shed?' goes Mum.

I suddenly remembered the ghost in the

window – it was Mr Kaminski, watching our early-morning comings and goings!

Dad went as red as the so-called strawberry on my pudding, which I had cunningly hidden under my spoon. Mr Kaminski realised too late that he had landed Dad in it.

As he didn't have any choice, Dad fessed up.

'I've been hiding in the shed until the coast was clear and then sneaking back inside for a snooze before you all got back.'

'But... you were all sweaty,' said Mum.

Dad didn't say anything. He just got the plant-sprayer from the cupboard under the sink, filled it with water and sprayed it all over his face and the front of his t-shirt. We gawped at him.

'I'm sorry,' he said, 'but all of you did it and that's the point of having guinea pigs. A great scientist doesn't test his ideas out on himself. He just writes down what he discovers... isn't that right, Mum?'

Gran wasn't being drawn in. Primrose flounced and tutted, and got up on the scales. Her mouth fell open. She hadn't lost any weight either. In fact, she had put some on.

'Oh, all right,' she said. 'You might as well know. Me and Peony have been hanging around in the cafe eating egg rolls when we were supposed to be jogging. But I haven't cheated at all otherwise except the bourbons in my bedroom. You can't sleep if you go to bed hungry.'

'I've got a whole box of berry oatcakes in my bedroom and I haven't touched one!' I couldn't help gloating as I stepped onto the scales.

'You've put on more weight than me, Miss Smug I-laid-off-the-oatcakes Peony!'

'But...'

'You had two breakfasts too,' Primrose said. 'What else?'

When you came to think about it, it was two of everything. Two breakfasts, two puddings at school, and two teas, what with having tea and cake with Gran at the Happy Haddock on the way home most afternoons.

'Yeah, but the trouble is, when you eat those tiny suppers and stuff you still feel hungry,' I protested. 'And you think about food all the time!'

'Oh dear,' said Mum, as she took her turn on the scales. It turned out she had been walking up to Stella's for toast and marmalade instead of jogging every morning.

'I did tell you I hated jogging,' she pointed out to Dad.

He was dumbfounded.

'I can't believe it,' he said, shaking his head.

We all looked at each other.

'I suppose we could try again?' suggested

Mum. She looked as keen as a cat that's got to go to the vet's.

'There's no time now,' Dad said. 'I'll just have to write the book anyway.'

'But your trial run didn't work,' said Gran.

Dad said people were always writing books without checking their ideas worked. 'What about the person who wrote "You can be a Millionaire"?' he said. 'If he really knew how to be a millionaire he wouldn't be bothering to write a book about it, would he? He'd be sipping champagne in his hammock on his own tropical island. Back me up, Viktor,' he said.

Mr Kaminski put on a puzzled look as if he had suddenly lost the ability to understand English.

'All right then – what about Daphne?' goes Dad. 'If she really knew "How to handle stress at work", do you think she'd have left the paper high and dry without an agony aunt?'

Dad said he wasn't going to let any of us tell him what he could or could not do.

'I am going to write my book!' he said.

Chapter 13
Gran on a mission and doggy depression

That night, I dreamt about this beautiful tepee, all covered in paintings of wild animals. When I tried to go into it, it turned into a huge pointy mountain. I leapt up the mountain like a sure-footed goat, all the way to the top, but before I had a chance to look at the view, the ruined tower from the top of Beacon Hill suddenly dropped out of the sky and squashed me flat.

Flat. That's how I felt all the next day, and it didn't help that Toby and Jess kept going on about orienteering. I had thought it was just a walk with a map, which didn't seem impossible, especially if it wasn't hilly. But it turned out it was more like a race. You worked out the next place you had to get to and then you ran as fast as you could to get there quicker than anyone else.

It wasn't surprising I didn't manage to get up Beacon Hill, considering I seemed to have got fat in four weeks instead of fit. But if I couldn't keep up with Toby and his family walking, how was I ever going to keep up with them running?

When I got home from school, Primrose was in her bedroom playing gloomy music, so she obviously hadn't sorted things out with Matt. There was a note from Mum on the counter.

Bo-o-o-o-ored! Gone to Stella's. Back in time to cook tea. Love, Mum.

There was also a weird, huffy note from Dad.

I might be a bit late. Going to the library on my way home from the office to collect some books I ordered. Yes, it's research for my book, and you can pick your chins up off the table. Dad.

The family organiser was completely empty after the Big Weekend. There wouldn't be any more ticks for sticking to the diet and doing our runs from now on, and there was nothing on it at all until Easter with Mum's drawing of an egg and my gold smiley next to 'Snowdon'.

I was just trying to decide whether or not to put 'midnight orienteering' on to break up the emptiness, when Gran arrived. She was on her way down to the Happy Haddock to see Jane. She said she was on a mission of mercy and wanted me to go with her.

'Jane's really worried about Magnus,' she said. 'The vet says he's depressed. Well, I told her, "You know who's a genius with dogs? My Peony! I'll get her to come down and see him after school."'

She glanced at the family organiser behind me.

'Dear, dear – it looks so bare,' she said. 'Still, I've got a good idea!'

Gran's always having good ideas, such as the time she set up a rescue centre for unwanted cockerels and upset the neighbours because they crowed half the night. Or the time she booked a flight to India and forgot to check whether her passport was up to date.

Gran stuck a bunch of smileys of all the colours on the family organiser and wrote, 'Gran's Grand House-warming Party!' next to them.

'We'll have it in four weeks because that will give me plenty of time to get the house nice and organise everything,' she said.

It was also the day after Toby's midnight orienteering, so it helped me to make up my mind. I couldn't go racing round the countryside all night and then help Gran to prepare for her big party. I'd probably fall asleep in the jelly.

You can't say no to Gran when she's on a mission so I got changed out of my school uniform and we walked down to the Happy Haddock together. She said Jane was hoping I'd have time to take Magnus for a walk because she was very busy herself and the vet said it would do him good to get out in the open air.

'You've got so much experience taking all sorts of dogs for a walk,' she said. 'You do it every Saturday at the kennels.'

I didn't like to point out that I had absolutely no experience of prising a big grumpy Labrador out of his hiding-place and dragging him off round the harbour, and to be honest it wasn't my idea of fun.

We didn't say the word 'walkies,' but Magnus spotted the lead and bolted under the bar. We tried to coax him out, then Jane hauled on his collar, but he wouldn't budge.

In the end we had to trick him with a chip. As

soon as he leaned out for it, Jane slipped the lead over his head.

Magnus gave Jane the evils as she pulled him to the door and pushed him out onto the street. You could see he wasn't depressed – no way! He was spoilt and bad-tempered, but I guessed that wasn't the kind of thing a vet could say to a dog owner.

'Thank you so much, Peony,' said Jane, handing me the lead. 'This is so kind of you.'

Like I had any choice.

'That's OK,' I said, trying to smile.

The walk was every bit as bad as I thought it would be. Magnus grunted and grumbled along for a couple of minutes, then sat down and gave me his you-can't-make-me look.

With a normal dog, you can talk to them. You can sit down and sort it out together, make friends, make him want to work with you. When I tried to talk to Magnus, he completely blanked me.

We limped round the harbour with me pulling and pushing him every time he ground to a halt, and then we started back towards the Happy Haddock. Magnus speeded up when he realised we were going home. By the time we got there, he was almost pulling me.

He dived under the nearest table and sat there glaring out at us.

'He looks much more cheerful now,' said Jane. Gran agreed.

'Would you like Peony to walk him every day? I'm sure she wouldn't mind!'

'Well, maybe just till he's starting to feel happier, yes please,' said Jane. 'That would be marvellous!'

I was doomed. We'd be in another ice age before miserable Magnus started to feel happier. He didn't want to be happy. He liked being mean and moody. It worked for him. It got him chips.

Gran didn't seem to notice that her plan to cure Magnus's depression was making me feel depressed. On the way home, she bought me a packet of dog stickers, all different breeds, in the paper shop.

'You can stick one on the family organiser every day when you've given Magnus his walk,' she said, with a big, wide, happy grin. 'Won't that be nice?'

Chapter 14
Life isn't fair
and Magnus doesn't care

I stuck a Springer Spaniel on the family organiser. There were fifty stickers in the pack. I just hoped Gran wasn't expecting me to get through all of them.

'What for you put dog on?' Mr Kaminski asked.

He was sitting at the kitchen table talking to Mum while she was cooking. First day back to normal meals, and Mr K couldn't even wait till it was ready before 'just so happening' to pop over.

'Jane wants me to walk Magnus every day,' I said. 'Gran landed me in it, and then she bought me these stickers.'

'You'll enjoy that,' Mum said. 'You like dogs.'

'It isn't dogs – it's Magnus.'

Mum changed the subject.

'We're having leeks-and-cheese tonight.'

She nodded towards five muddy leeks lined up on the kitchen counter. In case you're lucky enough never to have seen a leek, it's like a long thin onion, with lots of layers. Mum's leeks always come with extra crunch because she isn't good at getting the grit out.

There was a pile of potatoes, sprouts on a stalk, and a box of frozen blackberries beside them.

'Thank heavens for good friends,' Mum sighed. 'I was so bored not having any work to do, then Stella took me up to her allotment and gave me all these fresh veggies and blackberries from her freezer.'

I sat down on the rug and Dennis hopped over to me. He sniffed my feet for about ten hours, then rubbed his chin on them and jumped up onto my lap. I stroked his soft fur and velvety ears, which were always so much warmer than the rest of him.

Mr Kaminski said to Mum, 'You can help Stella with allotment until work comes?'

'I wish!' She started peeling the potatoes. 'The problem is, Stella's so on top of it, there's really nothing to do.'

Mum said, if only everyone kept on top of their gardening in the winter-time like Stella. 'People seem to forget they've even got gardens until it's hot enough to sit out in them.'

'Then you shall remind them, yes?'

Mr Kaminski said Mum and Stella should make some leaflets about Garden Angels and put one through every single letterbox in the town. He rummaged in his pocket and pulled out a crumpled leaflet about winter swimming sessions at the leisure centre.

'Leaflet like this, it comes today.'

Mr Kaminski said they could get Primrose to deliver them. It might take her mind off the Matt situation. He said Mum could pay her to do it.

'I think my daughter should be able to help out without being bribed,' said Mum.

'Ha!' I thought. 'She's going to love that!'

Dad came home with a bunch of library books and a face like thunder. It looked like he might still be cross with us for being such rotten guinea pigs, but it turned out the person he was cross with was Gran.

'She phoned me first thing this morning and made me go up there "on my way to work",' he grumbled. 'It isn't on my way to work. It isn't on anyone's way to anywhere!'

'What was the problem?' asked Mum, hacking at the leeks.

'A drippy tap!' said Dad. 'She wanted it sorted straight away before the party. "The party's not for ages," I said. "Can't it at least wait until the weekend?" But oh, no – I had to go down to Harbourside Stores right then and there and get a new washer.'

Dad being Dad, he got the wrong size of washer, and Gran asked him to stop by for another one in his lunch-break.

'I've been up and down to the blooming Harbourside Stores all blooming day,' he said. 'On a Monday! When I'm supposed to be in the office!'

Mum said Gran must be really grateful to have such a kind caring son. Dad scowled at her.

Mr Kaminski said no wonder she had a kind caring son – she was a very kind caring woman! Then Dad scowled at him.

Upstairs, Primrose's music suddenly stopped. Finally! She must have been playing gloomy tunes the whole time since she got home from school. We heard her slow footsteps on the stairs, and she made her best tragedy-queen entrance, staring down at her phone.

Mum said, 'Mr Kaminski has thought of a great way for me and Stella to drum up some business, Primrose.'

Primrose gave her the stare that says, 'and I'm interested – why?'

'We're going to make some leaflets. I thought you might like to deliver them for us.'

'You're joking, yeah?' said Primrose.

'No – it might be good for you to have a project to take your mind off Matt.'

Bad move. As soon as she heard the M-word, Primrose squealed like a piglet in pain. Mum panicked.

'We'll pay you, of course,' she said.

It was as if she had flicked off the squeal switch. Primrose thought about it. I didn't need to think.

'I'll do it!' I said.

Mum said I was too young to have that kind of responsibility and anyway, I didn't need extra pocket-money at my age. A bit of spare cash could help Primrose save up for something – a new dress, perhaps.

'Or, if she hasn't completely blown it with Matt, the same one in a bigger size,' I suggested.

I was only trying to be helpful but Primrose went off on one and I got the blame! Mum said, 'What's got into you today? How could you say something like that?'

'Well, it's not fair,' I said. 'I've got lumbered with walking Magnus for nothing, and now you're going to pay Primrose to deliver some leaflets.'

'Sorry, Peony – sometimes life just isn't fair,' said Mum, absent-mindedly picking up Mr Kaminski's leaflet. 'Swimming,' she pondered. 'I used to love that. I might give it a go until the work picks up.'

I was spitting feathers all the next day and by the time I got to Jane's I felt fit to explode. It didn't help when Magnus wedged himself behind the bar and we had to go through the whole chip palaver again, but at least once Jane had got the lead on him he seemed to submit. She didn't have to push and pull him out the door.

'I get it – you don't want to do this,' I muttered at him, through gritted teeth. 'Well, you're not the only one.'

He plodded along, head down, not stopping this time. You got the feeling he was just trying to get it over and done with as quickly as possible.

It was nothing like walking Sam. Sam's as blind as a bat and he's got stiff hips but he loves his walk. His nose goes into overdrive, and that makes you notice things, such as sweet peas in a tub and cigarette ends in the gutter, sunshine on a damp gate and rusty iron rings where the boats tie up.

Magnus wasn't listening to me but I talked to him anyway. I had to talk to someone and at least he was better than Mum, who got panicked into offering to pay Primrose for posting her leaflets, or Gran, who lumbered me with Magnus, or Dad, who had gone all weird, or Primrose, who gets everything on a plate from basically being a pain.

'It's not fair,' I said to Magnus's back. 'Mum says I can't be responsible for a bunch of stupid leaflets, but then they put me in charge of a big stroppy dog – no offense.'

Could leaflets slip their lead? I didn't think so! Could leaflets tread on a thorn, fling themselves at a cat or choke on a passing fly?

'Mum says Primrose needs extra pocket money. Why? To stop her going off on one. If she was a dog, she'd be just like you, Magnus. She'd be under the table in a massive sulk until somebody gave her a chip!'

I thought Magnus might not like being compared with Primrose, but he didn't care. He plod-plod-plodded on until we got to the look-out hut, and then he plod-plod-plodded back.

Chapter 15
Stickers and secret codes

Mum asked Primrose to write the number of leaflets she delivered each day on the family organiser, and at the end of the week, she would tot them up and work out what to pay.

On the first day, that number was twenty-three, which wasn't great considering that Polgotherick is a lot bigger than you think. There's a whole town of bungalows on the other side of the top road that you can't see from the harbour.

Mum said at that rate, by the time Primrose got round all the houses the summer would have come and gone, and so would all the gardening jobs. Primrose promised she would speed up. She had only been so slow on the first day because it was freezing cold and she had forgotten her hat and gloves.

'I would have turned into a block of ice if I'd stayed out there a second longer,' she said.

On the second day, the number dropped to twenty. Mum said maybe she should get someone to help her – a school friend, perhaps? The problem was, Primrose didn't really have any school friends. She was a one-friend-or-boyfriend-at-a-time kind of person. She had been joined at the hip with Mushy Marcus for months; then there was Bianca, and straight after her, there was Matt.

'It's a shame you still haven't sorted things out with Matt,' said Mum. 'He would be happy to help you.'

Primrose said how could she sort things out with Matt? It was too late now. It would be too embarrassing to even try!

'OK, well, here's the thing,' said Mum. 'If you think you've offended someone, act like nothing's happened. Text Matt just as if things are completely normal between you.'

Primrose looked confused. I was feeling puzzled myself – weren't you supposed to say sorry if you'd been a pain?

'Ask him over. Say you're missing him,' Mum suggested. 'Tell him you wish you had given him a chance to explain why he didn't bring Sam the other day. Say you can see now that it was because the weather wasn't warm enough, and it would be much more sensible to recreate your first date on your nine-month anniversary, when it's warmer!'

You could see Primrose thinking about it. You could almost hear her brain ticking over. Eventually, she said, 'Maybe that *is* why he didn't bring Sam.'

Primrose sent the text. Matt was round our house in less than an hour. She was so right, he declared. That was exactly why he hadn't brought Sam, and he should have explained. Primrose stuck one of her red smileys on the family organiser and wrote 'Matt and Primrose – nine months anniversary' beside it.

After that, Primrose's leaflet-count went right up. It was still freezing cold – 'too cold for snow,' everyone said – but they had love to keep them warm. She actually said that! Whenever Primrose falls out with a boyfriend and makes up again, the mush-factor goes through the roof.

119

By the time Matt got to our house every day it was already getting dark, so they ended up delivering the leaflets by moonlight. After the last leaflet was delivered, they went for a walk on the beach to celebrate, and Matt gave her the silver necklace. Primrose said it was sooo romantic.

They decided to keep going out for moonlit walks even though they didn't have any leaflets left, and instead of numbers on the family organiser, they drew a star for every night-time walk. At least it wasn't hearts and kisses.

When Primrose is a pain, she's appalling, but when she's in love she's really nice. She doesn't keep going off the deep end over nothing, plus she talks to me.

'On frosty nights, the stars are really twinkly. Matt says they're like my eyes,' she said.

She attempted a twinkle but I couldn't quite see it. I was thinking about midnight orienteering. That would have been my chance to go out at night, under the twinkly starry sky.

'Are you all right?' said Primrose.

I told her I was supposed to be going midnight orienteering with Toby's family and Jess, but it was the night before Gran's party so I'd decided not to go.

'Don't be daft,' Primrose said. 'You can have a lie-in and get up at lunch-time. You'll be fine.'

I straight away saw she was right – that excuse didn't hold up at all. So I had to tell her the truth about Beacon Hill, how I just plain couldn't keep up. Orienteering was like a race, I said. If I couldn't keep up with them walking, how was I ever going to keep up running?

Primrose said, if I had never been orienteering, how could I really know what it was like? You might get lots of rests. It might be easy! She stuck one of my gold smileys on the family organiser and wrote 'Midnight orienteering' next to it.

'Stop worrying,' she said. 'What's the worst that could happen?'

'What's the worst that could happen?' was the sort of thing that Dad might say, if he wasn't too busy grumbling about Gran. She was driving him mad, making him do odd jobs, fetching and carrying. She was determined to get Nash House looking like something off Your Perfect Home before the big party.

'I've got a full-time job,' he complained. 'Just because I work at home most of the time, that doesn't mean I can drop everything and be at her beck and call. I preferred it when she lived in St Ives!'

Mum said, was he perhaps making a mountain out of a molehill?

Dad was exasperated.

'Well, let's see,' he said. 'I'll draw a triangle on the family organiser every time she makes me go up there. We can decide whether it's a mountain or a molehill when we see how many there are!'

'Talking about the family organiser,' goes Mum, 'what do all those tens mean?'

Dad had been writing tens on every day beside my dog sticker and Primrose's leaflet-count and stars.

'Pages,' Dad said. 'I'm trying to write ten pages of my book every day, but what with Gran's shenanigans, I have to write in the night sometimes to hit my target.'

Considering the way he cheated by hiding when he should have been running, the surprising thing was, I believed him. I said that to Magnus when we were walking. 'My dad's acting weird,' I said. 'He's actually getting up in the middle of the night sometimes to make his ten pages. Whatever happened to "When the going gets tough, there's always TV?"'

Magnus still didn't seem the slightest bit interested, but at least he had stopped being grumpy with me since the first few walks. It started with a grudging flick of his tail when I arrived at the Happy Haddock on the third day. By the end of the first week, he was actually sitting in the doorway, waiting for me.

By the end of the second week, Magnus had stepped up a gear from plodding to trotting, and Jane said he had a real spring in his step. By the end of the third week, I actually found I was looking forward to taking him out for his walk.

The family organiser was filling up with dog stickers, leaflet numbers, stars, tens and triangles, as well as Mum's green smileys for her swimming sessions. Then someone phoned about the leaflet and offered her a job clearing one of the steep gardens behind the houses in Ship Lane, and building some terraces. It was a big job because Ship Lane isn't really a lane but a path, so you couldn't get a mechanical digger in.

'Next weekend's going to be a good one!' she said happily, putting her green sticker beside my orienteering and Gran's party.

I hoped she was right. I mean, in answer to Primrose's question, the worst that could happen would be if I couldn't keep up, and that meant our team fell behind. Toby's family is lots of fun and really, really nice – but they really, seriously do not like coming last.

Chapter 16
Geared up to go
and the moon on the snow

In Finland, they've got forty words for snow. I saw that on The Plight of the Polar Bears. Here in Polgotherick, we've only got one, and we hardly ever use it.

For weeks, it had been trying to snow but not managing. Then, the very day me and Mum didn't want it to, it succeeded. It was only flecks at first, floating in the glow of light from the kitchen window.

'I hope this doesn't get worse,' Mum said, peering out into the darkness. 'The ground's too frozen for Stella and me to do any digging, but at least if the snow holds off we'll be able to clear the site.'

They weren't supposed to start until nine o'clock but she was so happy to finally have some work, she couldn't wait, so she left the house at quarter to seven. I got ready to go to the kennels. If we had lots of snow, me and Becky could build a snowman when we had finished cleaning the pens and walking the dogs. That would be brilliant!

But on the other hand, would lots of snow mean that midnight orienteering might be cancelled? That would be horrible now I'd geared myself up to it, although at least if it was cancelled I couldn't mess it up, like Beacon Hill.

'Why the frown?' said Dad.

I blinked. Then I blinked again but he was still there.

'It's Saturday!' I said. 'It's not even seven o'clock yet.'

'I know.' He picked up a pen to write on the family organiser. 'I got up at five to finish my ten pages.'

Dad's triangles had turned out to be mountains rather than molehills. There was a whole range of them filling up the month of February, and it was getting worse every day. The closer we got to the house-warming party, the more Gran was making Dad run up and down.

The previous day, she had sent him down to the Harbourside Stores with a list of food for the party and then, when he'd walked all the way down there and back up again, she made him go back for some cocktail sticks because she had forgotten to put them on the list.

She had been doing that all week. Dad said why couldn't he go to the cash-and-carry on the edge of town instead? At least then he could take the car. But Gran wouldn't hear of it. Her grandmother had done all her shopping at the Harbourside Stores; her mother had always shopped there too. 'Use it or lose it,' she said.

Dad's mobile rang. He took it out of his dressing-gown pocket and squinted at the screen. You could tell it was Gran. I heard him saying, 'Yes... yes, that's fine... OK... Well, I'll have to shower and get dressed first...'

I put my hat and gloves on, and gave him a wave goodbye as I went out the door. There was thick frost on the zig-zag path that sparkled under the street lights, and specks of snow in the air. By the time I met Becky outside her house, the snowflakes had got bigger, though there still weren't many of them, but as we arrived at the kennels they stopped.

It didn't snow any more all day. Mum would be pleased. Dad would pleased too, as he was bound to be out and about fetching and carrying for Gran. Primrose was holed-up in the living-room with Matt. They had a day's worth of DVDs and chocs, so she wouldn't notice either way.

There was no-one around to talk to in the afternoon so I went down to the Happy Haddock to take Magnus for a walk. It was OK talking to Magnus now that I had given up expecting him to listen. It only occurred to me when I was slogging back up the zig-zag path two hours later that it probably wasn't the best idea to spend virtually the whole day walking dogs when I was going to need a super-lot of energy for running round all night.

At ten o'clock, when I would normally be in bed, Dad walked up to the top road with me. The frost on the path crunched under our feet. There wasn't a single star up above, nor any sign of the moon. Dad said that was because of the snow clouds covering the sky. After all that build-up from Primrose, it felt like a bit of a let-down.

I had three pairs of socks on under my wellies, two pairs of gloves, a hat and scarf and a back-pack full of my overnight things. Jess and me were staying at Toby's because we didn't want to wake our families up, coming home at three in the morning.

As we drove out of Polgotherick, it started to full-on snow. You couldn't see anything outside the car windows but white. Toby's dad put the wipers on and slowed right down. He and Toby's mum talked about turning back, but Toby and Leah begged them not to.

Jess was looking as nervous as I felt, though probably not for the same reason. I couldn't tell if my legs really had turned into lead weights, or if I was imagining it. I definitely wasn't worried about getting stranded in the snow because Toby's parents were bound to have packed plenty of emergency blankets and rations.

Toby's mum phoned the organisers and they said enough people were already there to start the event, so it wouldn't matter if we were a bit late. She explained to Jess and me that it wasn't like a regular race where you all have to set off together. The teams set off one after another and were timed individually. The one that recorded the fastest time at the end was the winner.

I still didn't really understand how it worked. I just clocked the worrying words 'race' and 'winner'. When we finally got out of the car, our feet sank up to our ankles in snow. I suddenly remembered the tough trudge through the pine needles in the woods at the bottom of Beacon Hill.

'How did the snow get so deep so quickly?' I said.

'It's probably been snowing up here on and off all day,' said Jess. 'You always get more snow away from the sea, especially on high ground.'

Toby's dad gave us head-torches and we set off down a track from the far side of the car park. It was dark, but the snow gave everything an eerie glow. It stuck to the trunks and branches of the trees on either side, making them look like ghost-trees, reaching out.

We could hardly see any distance into the woods, but you could tell they weren't like the little woods at Beacon Hill. The trees were huge and the tracks were wide, and it felt like you could walk forever and never reach the other side.

After a few minutes we saw a glimmer of light up ahead and, coming closer, made out a camping table under a row of lanterns hanging from a rope between the trees. There were people milling around. Toby's dad signed our team up and got our map and stuff.

We had to find ten places, in the right order. They were called control points. He showed us where they were on the map. Each one would be marked by an orange and white flag. I peered into the darkness between the trees and wondered how we were ever going to find them.

Toby's mum and dad did the map-reading while the rest of us pretended to understand how they did it and went in the direction they pointed. We all wanted to be the first one to spot the flag.

We hadn't even found the first one when an owl hooted close by and Jess jumped out of her skin. She grabbed hold of my arm. She wouldn't let go. She isn't an outdoors kind of person even in the daytime, and she's scared of all wild animals, including toads. Seriously. Even though she knows five facts about them, number one being that they don't have any teeth.

It was like being in a three-legged race with Jess clinging onto me, but we still managed to find four of the flags before Toby and Leah. We raced around the dark woods, stopping every few minutes to read the map, waiting for directions. Other people's torches bobbed in the darkness round about. We heard their voices through the trees. We had no idea which control point they were looking for, or who was making the fastest time.

When we finally got back to the start-point and recorded our finish time, I couldn't believe it. We had been running around in the woods for two whole hours! I didn't even feel tired. I could have done it all again.

It turned out I was wrong about Toby's family; we didn't win, but they didn't mind. 'It's the taking part that counts,' said Toby's dad. 'Did you enjoy it?'

Did I enjoy it? It was the best night ever, even if we didn't see the sparkling stars or the moon. But as we walked back down the wide track towards the car, the clouds parted, and there it was, half-full, silver-white, dazzling bright. It seemed to float up into the sky.

The moon lit up the snow, casting shadows under the trees, as dark as sun-shadows. We grinned at each other in the sudden light, seeing every detail of our faces, even the pinkness of our cheeks.

'Me and Leah put the tepee up again this afternoon,' said Toby. 'Shall we sleep in it tonight?'

I grinned, and I couldn't stop grinning, all the way back in the car.

Chapter 17
The best books and the body you want

You know when your Gran has a huge house-warming party and you think, 'If a single nother person says how much I've grown I'm going to make a break for it and build a snowman in the garden?'

But then the guests go, and it's just your family and your sister's boyfriend, and Mr Kaminski from next door, and Jane and Magnus from the Happy Haddock, sitting around amongst the dirty dishes, and you're really glad you didn't?

Well, that's what happened to me because, all of a sudden, things started to get interesting.

Mum said, 'That was a peach of a party!'

Dad said so it should be, considering the amount of effort that went into it.

'Not that I minded helping, of course, but it was tough trying to get Nash House up to Your Perfect Home standards at the same time as doing a full-time job and writing a book.'

'Yes,' Gran said. 'Sorry about that.'

She glanced at Mr Kaminski and they both got this really shifty look.

'Is there something you aren't telling us?' said Dad.

'W-e-ell... not really,' said Gran. 'I mean... I don't want you to be cross!'

Outside the big bay window, it was starting to get dark. The snow had lost its dazzle and the sea looked steely-grey. Gran had plumped for a lunchtime party because she wanted her guests to see Nash House in all its day-time glory, with its freshly painted outside walls, new windows and front door.

'Your mother is wonderful, kind woman,' Mr Kaminski said to Dad. 'Always, she only trying to help.'

Dad looked at Gran. He raised his eyebrows. She took a deep breath.

'It was after your weigh-in,' she said. 'Your fitness plan didn't seem to be quite working but you said you didn't have time to bother about that – you just had to get on and write the book.'

Mr Kaminski said that although some books, such as, for example, Daphne's "How to handle stress at work," were obviously not based on proper research, the best ones were.

'And we are wanting your book should be one of best ones,' he said.

'So we decided to adjust your ideas and do our own test-run,' said Gran. 'We came up with a plan about how to get fit in four weeks, then I set the date for my party for four weeks' time, and we got started.'

Dad said, with respect, it was a well-known fact that there were only two main aspects to getting fit and those were diet and exercise. If his test-run hadn't got the right results, that might be down to the quality of his guinea pigs. No offense!

'I know,' said Gran. 'That's why we used the same guinea pigs.'

We all looked at each other.

Gran said, when it came to diet, fitness was not the same as thinness. It was no good starving yourself stick-thin and being as weak as a wafer – that wasn't the kind of body you would want.

It was about being a healthy weight, and the best way to achieve that was by eating a healthy diet.

One thing you could say for Mum's nutritious yet adventurous cooking was that there was always plenty of fresh fruit and veg.

'That's why none of you really had a weight problem in the first place,' she said.

'This dinner-in-box is very bad,' said Mr Kaminski. 'Is too small, always you are hungry. You eat many, many snacks. You get fatter.'

Primrose pointed out that she had actually been nearly too fat to do up her summer dress when all this started, but Gran said not fitting into a skimpy little dress didn't exactly make her an elephant.

You could see the light-bulb flick on above Matt's head.

'Is that why you cancelled our six-month anniversary?'

Primrose was sitting on his lap. Any sensible person would have thrown her off.

'I couldn't even do it up by then,' Primrose protested, as if it was a perfectly reasonable explanation. 'We'd just done Dad's get-fit-in-four-weeks-plan.'

Matt gave her a massive hug. He said she could put on fifty kilos and dress like a bag of potatoes, she would always look beautiful to him.

'There's no-one in the world like you!' he said. He got that bit right, anyway.

Gran said that, with Mum cooking again so we didn't go pigging out on crisps and bicks between meals, she and Mr Kaminski reckoned our diet was sorted.

'So then we thought about exercise, and we asked ourselves why going for a jog every day before breakfast hadn't worked. We decided it must be because you didn't really want to do it.'

Mum muttered that she had, in fact, told Dad at the outset that she didn't like jogging. Primrose said she didn't see how anyone could like jogging or any other form of exercise for that matter, if it meant getting out of bed an hour before you had to.

'The thing about exercise is it's hard,' said Gran. 'You've got to want to do it, and that means it's got to be something you enjoy. So we thought, "What would Primrose enjoy? Making a bit of extra pocket-money!"'

'Is why I say to Jan, make leaflets, ask Primrose to deliver,' said Mr Kaminski.

'It was an unexpected bonus when Primrose and Matt got back together and found they liked walking on the beach by moonlight,' said Gran.

'And leaving that leaflet from the leisure centre,' Mum said. 'How cunning was that? You knew I was feeling bored and I've always loved swimming.'

Gran grinned at her. Mr Kaminski looked pleased with himself.

'Also we think, what will Peony enjoy? Is dogs!'

I looked at Jane. 'So the vet didn't really say Magnus was depressed?'

She shook her head.

'But he must have been, because look at him now. He's like a different dog!'

'Another unexpected bonus,' said Gran.

Magnus sat up. He knew we were talking about him. I stroked him and he wagged his tail. Jane said she might take up walking him herself now. It might help her to trim down too.

'Does that mean you won't need me any more?' I said. I was surprised how disappointed I felt. Plus, if walking Magnus every day was what got me fit enough to go orienteering, I had to keep it up. Then, by Easter-time, climbing up Snowdon would be a piece of cake!

'Not at all,' said Jane. 'Two walks are better than one for Magnus and anyway, if I discover that I don't enjoy it I'll find excuses not to do it, like your gran says.'

'But what about Dad?' said Primrose. 'He doesn't really like any exercise except football, and he's on the bench.'

Gran said that for the slightly more lazy person such as Dad, exercise had to be not so much enjoyable as unavoidable. That's why she'd had him running up and down to the Harbourside Stores for her on endless errands, and doing strenuous jobs around the house.

Dad isn't the sort of person who holds a grudge – he can't be bothered. He grinned at Gran.

'Well, it worked!' he said. 'Ray's just told me I'm back on the team.'

Dad's team coach, Ray, had been at the party, along with half the population of Polgotherick.

'It worked for me too,' Primrose said. 'When I was deciding what to wear this morning, I tried on my anniversary dress... and it fits!'

'And I can keep up with Stella again,' said Mum. 'Clearing that garden yesterday, she was the one who had to take the first break.'

I joined in. 'I had to run around for two whole hours when we went orienteering, and I didn't get tired at all.'

Gran and Mr Kaminski looked delighted. Now Dad would just have to make a few small tweaks to his book and all the ideas would be properly tried-and-tested. The key to fitness was healthy meals and exercise you enjoyed.

Dad shook his head. He said he had discovered that writing a book was like doing exercise – it was harder than you thought. You wouldn't do it unless you really wanted to.

'I found I really didn't want to write a book about fitness – especially not after it turned out my ideas didn't seem to work.'

'But what about all those tens?' I said.

Dad said, 'Oh, I have been writing a book, only not about fitness. I spotted a paperback called, "Slow down, chill out", when I was at the library and I thought, "I could write a book like that!" After all, I'm always trying to stop you lot getting your knickers in a knot and I've spent my whole life testing out my ideas!'

Dad said the title of each chapter was one of his mottoes. Chapter one was called, 'Better late than having to set the alarm.' Chapter two was 'Nature abhors a vacuum cleaner.' Then there was 'If a job's worth doing, it's worth getting someone else to do it' and 'If at first you don't succeed, give up.' The second-to-last chapter was, 'He who hesitates might get out of doing things,' and the last one was, 'When the going gets tough, there's always TV.'

'Ed thinks that should be the title of the book. I emailed it to him yesterday. He loves it – he says it's going to make our fortune!'

Dad said people had never understood him. Everyone thought he was lazy, or joking around.

They didn't understand that doing as little work as possible and maxing out on chill-time was a perfectly reasonable choice.

'You've got to decide what's important to you,' he said. 'Well, for me, the most important thing is having plenty of time for sports, mates and my three best girls.'

That took the wind out of our sails. It was as if we were seeing him for the first time.

'What?' said Dad.

Jane gave herself a little shake.

'This calls for a celebration,' she said. 'Supper at the Happy Haddock – my treat!'

Gran said she would have loved to, but she and Mr Kaminski had plans.

'It's a good job this top isn't too tight,' she said. 'I may need to fit into it again in six months' time.'

They were going on a date! My gran and Mr Kaminski, who were both a million squillion years old.

'This is New Year wish I could not tell,' Mr Kaminski said, with a happy sigh.

The rest of us walked down to the Happy Haddock. It was snowing, big soft floaty flakes. When we got down to the harbour, we built a snowman right outside Jane's pub. Then we played snowballs until our fingers froze.

But after four weeks on Gran's secret fitness plan, not one of us felt tired at all.

Have you read all the Peony Pinker books?

How to get what you want by Peony Pinker
978-1-4081-3287-6

How to get the family you want by Peony Pinker
978-1-4081-3286-9

How to get the friends you want by Peony Pinker
978-1-4081-5236-2

By Jenny Alexander

Published by A&C Black
£5.99